To Jamie

BETWEEN A ROCK
&
A Hot Mess

THE SINCLAIR BRIDES
BOOK ONE

PHYLLIS BOURNE

All my best! Phyllis

Red Lipstick Press
Cover by Earthly Charms
Edited by B. Williams

ISBN: 978-0-9913490-2-9

Interior format by The Killion Group
http://thekilliongroupinc.com

CHAPTER 1

RILEY

An unladylike snort escaped from between my lips, earning a frown from my sister.

"Oh, Riley." Hope shook her head, sighed, and tsked me.

The way my family tossed it around, you would think the word Oh accompanied by a disapproving huff was my name. Actually, it's Riley Sinclair, and I did not gloat.

Okay, maybe I had just a bit, but under the circumstances, who could blame me? The man was annoying as hell and had deserved everything I could dish out, and more. "It's called w-i-n-n-i-n-g." I spelled the word out slowly in an attempt to school my sister on how to handle a victory, but it was a wasted effort.

Still, nothing could steal the triumphant thrill of Sinclair Construction's softball team handing Mills Plumbing their ass this evening in a seven-to-two beatdown. I glanced around the dining room of First Down sports bar, where my crew was enjoying celebratory bottles of beer as they awaited pizza and wings on the company tab. Then I met my sister's sanctimonious side-eye.

"We weren't even playing Parker Construction. Hudson Parker was only there to watch the game."

Hope threw up her hands. She didn't play on the company team, thank God. However, she still came out to cheer us on. "You had no call whatsoever to go bulldozing into the stands to rub his nose in the win. It was unprofessional and unsportsmanlike, not to mention a totally ungracious move on your part."

Ungracious. I rolled my eyes so hard they nearly bounced off the ceiling. "I'm reserving my nonexistent manners for tea with the queen. As far as being unprofessional goes, we're off the clock. So there's nothing wrong with letting the head of Parker Construction know he can expect the same kind of whipping if our teams face off in the championship game."

My sister sticking up for the enemy was even more irksome than her criticism of my so-called unsportsmanlike behavior. "Besides, I'm the boss. Who's going to check me?"

"You're so rude." Hope shuddered and took a sip from her lemon-adorned glass of mineral water. "If Mom had witnessed your bad behavior, she would have checked you, all right." She leveled a glossy French-manicured fingertip in my direction. "You may run the work crews, Riley Sinclair, but she owns the company and is therefore the boss of you."

Well, she had me there. All I could do was grunt and take a swig of my beer. Hope and our mother sat behind desks in the air-conditioned offices of our company's headquarters. What did they know? Neither of them were outdoors on the front line checking on our various job sites around town. Not once had they ever had to swing a hammer or take the wheel of a backhoe.

"Besides, it's only a stupid game," she continued. "The point of the company participating in recreational league sports is to foster camaraderie and have fun."

"Just a game?"

I stared at my sister slack-jawed before looking down at my jersey, dirt-stained from my dive for home plate. I zeroed in on the red, green, and white emblem of the company started by our late father. Like a talisman, it reinforced the lessons on competitiveness and killer instinct he'd ingrained in me as the oldest of his daughters.

I was about to remind my prim-and-proper sibling how important our company's softball and bowling teams and *winning* had been to him when the waitress placed a large pizza in the center of the table.

Hope topped our plates with the first slices before I could grab mine. I used my hands to lift a topping-laden slice from my half to my mouth. My sister unwrapped cutlery from a napkin, and then began to cut her slice from the cheese-only side of the pizza into perfect bite-size portions. No matter how many times I'd watched her do it, the sight of Hope eating pizza, buffalo wings, and even hamburgers with a knife and fork always threw me.

Silence reigned at the table as we spent the next few moments focusing on our food. Despite our differences, the one thing the Sinclair sisters had in common were healthy appetites and a deep appreciation of mealtime.

After downing two slices, I reached for another and got back to the topic at hand. "This was way more than just a game. It's a point of pride, and so was rubbing Hudson Parker's nose in it."

Hope shrugged. "The guy seems okay to me, and not too bad on the eyes. If you weren't so busy complaining about him, you might notice that the man is fine."

"Ha!" I practically barked. "Yeah, he's fine, all right. Fine with trying to steal business from us. Fine with taking the food right out of our mouths."

Hope eyed me over the rim of her water

glass as she took a sip. "Nashville is booming. There's enough new construction going on here to provide business and food for all of us. Besides, business isn't what's got you so worked up, and you know it. You're still mad Parker Construction won last year's first-place softball trophy, as well as last fall's bowling league championship."

"Both those bowling and softball trophies had been in Sinclair Construction's hands for years, before his company showed up in town and pulled together teams," I argued.

"*Winning* teams," Hope amended.

A fact that continued to rankle me. "He'd better savor those past victories, because they're the only ones he's going to get. And there's absolutely nothing wrong with warning him that our team is coming for that ass."

"Riley!" Hope admonished.

"It's the truth."

"Lighten up, Riley. You too, Miss Priss." The metallic jangle of bracelets accompanied a familiar voice, as our friend, Plum, plopped down in the empty chair at our table and adjusted her gauzy, tie-dye skirt.

Sugar Plum Watson (her government name) had grown up next door to us and knew the Sinclair sisters nearly as well as we knew each other. She also refused to hold a conversation with anyone who called her by her first name.

Plum shrugged her tote bag off her

shoulder onto the floor and helped herself to pizza, not bothering with a plate. She signaled the waitress and ordered a diet cola and a salad before turning her attention to me. "How'd the game go?"

"We won."

"Good," she nodded. "We won't have to listen to your sore loser bellyaching all evening."

"But I'm not a sore..."

The matching looks on Plum and Hope's faces stopped me midsentence. I can argue with the best of them, but not when I'm dead wrong. I relayed the game highlights to Plum, who appeared more interested in the salad the waitress had slid in front of her than my softball game.

"This win puts us one step closer to getting that trophy back," I said.

"You mean closer to shoving it in Hudson Parker's face," Hope clarified.

Plum looked up from her salad, fork poised midair. "Who's he?"

"A guy on another team Riley was rude to earlier."

Plum smirked. "Riley, rude. What else is new?"

"I know, right?" my sister asked rhetorically, and they shared a laugh at my expense.

"Oh, I have something to show you." Plum abandoned her food, reached into her tote bag and retrieved a magazine. The thick glossy landed on the table with a thud.

I caught sight of the cover. A woman with a death grip on a pink bouquet stared up from it. She was swathed in white satin and her teeth shone like high beams on a dark road.

Plum flipped through the pages of the bridal magazine, stopping on one she'd flagged with a Post-it note. She shoved it in my sister's direction. "I think these bridesmaid dresses are exactly what you've been looking for."

Hope's eyes went soft as she looked at the magazine, and her face took on the expression she wore whenever anything to do with her upcoming nuptials came up. "Oh, my God, they're gorgeous."

I averted my gaze from the page of pale-pink dresses, hoping the twinge of envy I felt deep down wasn't visible. With the recent engagements of Hope and Plum, it seemed as if everyone I knew was now engaged, married, or cohabiting with a significant other in a state of domestic bliss.

Plum commandeered the magazine and flipped to another flagged page. "And I think something like this might work for my wedding gown." She pointed to a model wearing a dress so frothy it looked like whipped cream, and then to the red dresses beside it. "Maybe these for my bridesmaids, seeing as how we're having a Christmas holiday wedding."

"What?" Hope's mouth dropped open. "I thought you had your heart set on autumn."

Plum launched into a lengthy explanation. It wasn't exactly a surprise to learn her future mother-in-law had demanded the change and her son had followed suit. "Doug wants to make his mom happy, and when you're part of a couple, you have to compromise." Tension marred her forced smile as she pointed to a green lace dress. "Or maybe this one for the bridesmaids?"

I unleashed a yawn that pretty much summed up my feelings on the subject. "Come on, you two aren't going to ruin my softball victory with a bunch of talk about dresses and wedding whatnot, are you?"

The smile Hope wore while ogling the pages of the magazine turned into a frown when she looked up at me. "You might want to pay attention to this *whatnot*, since you're the maid of honor in both of our weddings and will be wearing these dresses."

"Humph." I sat back in my chair and took another swig of beer.

"Oh, Riley," Hope chastised. She shook her head as she reached for her mineral water.

Plum, on the other hand, wasn't fooled by my show of bravado. I averted my eyes hoping to shield my thoughts, but it was too late.

My friend stretched an arm across the table and covered my free hand with hers. "Your turn will come, Riley," she said softly.

"Oh, no. I'm not looking to have my life revolve around some man's whims. Y'all can have that." I tried to pull my hand away to brush off her observation, but she tightened her grip.

Plum's perceptive gaze, the same one that had peered at me through countless birthday and slumber parties, knew better. She knew how it hurt me to always be the girl that boys thought of as a friend, but never a girlfriend. She knew that although I was happy for her and my sister, it would be tough for me to watch them both get married next year, when I didn't even have a prospect.

"There's a guy out there for you," she continued. "One who will appreciate how independent and capable you are, and absolutely adore you."

"She'd probably scare him off with her total lack of tact," Hope interjected.

She had a point. Men who weren't turned off by the fact I didn't look like the women who were currently in vogue—petite, waif thin, spackled in makeup with plastic boobs and a weave hanging down to my backside—didn't like my outspokenness. Nor had I met one that made me want to refrain from breaking off some real talk where I thought it was needed.

Plum shook her head. "I disagree," she said. "Riley's true Prince Charming will love everything about her, including her occasional obnoxiousness."

My longtime friend's words managed to slip through the tough hide of my defenses. I cleared my throat. "Do you really think so?"

What I had said before was true. I would never be the kind of woman whose life revolved around providing her man with a lifetime of maid and nanny service. Nor did I envy Plum's choice of a mama's boy, or the cheap bastard Hope had selected to be my future brother-in-law.

I didn't even want a big, splashy wedding. Still, I couldn't help but wonder if I'd ever have my own happily-ever-after...

Plum patted my hand before finally releasing it. "Of course you will," she said, as if she'd read my mind. "It's only a matter of time before you encounter a man who recognizes how utterly fabulous you are and we're all eating red velvet cake pops at your wedding reception."

The mention of my favorite dessert paled in comparison to the sparkle of the diamond solitaire on her left hand.

"If she doesn't bite his head off first." Something caught Hope's attention, and she looked beyond me toward the sports bar's front door. "Speak of the devil. It looks like one of your favorite victims just walked in."

"Who?" Plum and I asked simultaneously, both turning in our chairs toward the door.

Hudson Parker. What was he doing here?

"Damn," Plum said in a hushed tone. "If I

wasn't engaged, I wouldn't mind taking a bite out of him."

"He's quite handsome in a rugged kind of way," Hope chimed in.

I swiveled in my seat, refusing to look at him a second longer than necessary. "What he is, is a giant pain in my ass."

"Well, don't look now, big sister, but that ache in your posterior is headed this way."

"Every fine inch of him," Plum murmured. "What is he, six-three, six-four?"

"Definitely, six-four," Hope said.

"Shouldn't you be focused on your fiancé's height?" I snapped at my sister.

A long shadow loomed over the table. I scowled at its owner, while the two engaged women surrounding me stared up at him in awestruck, Idris Elba–worthy wonder. They were going gaga at the sight of Hudson Parker, of all people. Unbelievable. I resisted the urge to stick my finger down my throat.

"Evening, ladies."

Plum sighed at the sound of his deep baritone. A simpering little smile graced my prissy sister's lips.

"Riley." He inclined his head in my direction. The gesture made it clear the first greeting was reserved for the other two women at the table.

"What do you want, Parker?"

"Riley!" Hope scolded, but she was wasting her breath.

Arching a brow, I crossed my arms over

my chest and waited for his answer. He may have lulled by sister and best friend into a trance with those broad shoulders and muscles straining against the confines of his black T-shirt. Or maybe it was the chiseled face, square jaw, and skin baked to a deep shade of bronze by the sun.

It didn't affect me. I worked with his type all day long, so I wasn't as easily taken in or impressed. "Well?" I prodded.

"Can't a guy just come over and say hello?" he asked. "It's not as if we're strangers."

"We're not friends, either. I've already said all I have to say to you today, so why don't you...Ow!" A sharp pain in my leg that felt like a kick stopped me midsentence. I knew the sensible heel of Hope's pump was the culprit. "What did you kick me for?" I rubbed the sore spot where her shoe had connected with my shin.

She ignored the question. Meanwhile, Plum introduced herself and motioned toward the empty chair between us. "Would you like to join us, Mr. Parker?"

He ran his tongue over his full bottom lip before biting down on it with even white teeth, as if he were actually contemplating it. I guess the fact that if he had his way, Sinclair Construction would be out of business was lost on my best friend and sister.

Hope flashed him one of her polite, proper smiles. "There's plenty of pizza," she coaxed.

I leveled the man with a stare, so he'd know exactly what I thought of the idea. He may have had everyone else at the table mesmerized, but not me. "Too bad I can't fart right now."

"Riley!" My sister gasped.

Plum's face contorted into a frown. "Aw, Riley. We're trying to eat here."

In contrast, an amused smile touched Parker's lips and traveled up to his dark-brown eyes. I suppressed a pulse of awareness between my thighs that made me forget about the pain still radiating from my shin.

What the hell?

Hope and Plum's silliness must be contagious, I reasoned. No way anything about this man could turn me on.

"Perhaps, another time, ladies." He was talking to them, but his gaze remained on me. I held it without blinking, hoping to convey the message that I wasn't intimidated by him. *Or attracted.* "See you around, Riley."

"The next thing you'll see is the sight of one of my home-run balls sailing over your head," I said. "That is, if Parker Construction even makes the playoffs."

His smile deepened at the taunt, revealing a dimple in his left cheek. "Oh, we'll make the playoffs, all right. In fact, I'm confident the league's first-place trophy will remain in my office for another year," he said. "Be nice, and I may let you visit it."

"Riley be nice? Fat chance of that happening," Hope said as he walked away.

Both her and Plum's eyeballs were glued to his jean-clad behind as he sauntered across the room to join some of my crew, as well as players from Mills Plumbing, who were all watching a baseball game at the bar.

I snapped my fingers to rouse them from their trance and pointed to the wedding magazine they'd been poring over before the interruption. "Too bad your husbands-to-be aren't around to see you two bridezillas ogling ass."

"I-I was doing no such thing," Hope stammered in a weak protest. "Just because I don't act like I was raised in a barn, like you."

"Moo," I deadpanned.

Plum pointed a finger in Parker's direction. I followed it, relieved to see his back was to us. The last thing I wanted was for the man to think he was the topic of any conversation I participated in.

"Now *that*, Riley, is Prince Charming material," she said.

Unfortunately, I'd picked that moment to take a sip from my beer. "W-what?" I sputtered incredulously. "You must have lost your damn mind."

Hope nodded. "I'm inclined to agree with my sister for a change. She can't stand him."

"Are you blind?" Plum directed her question at me. "That man is hot. What do you have against tall, dark, and delicious anyway?"

I grunted. "More like slick, annoying, and ruthless. Besides, he's the competition. The man stole two big jobs from us."

"Sinclair Construction never had those jobs," Hope corrected. "His company won those bids fair and square."

"We would have if he hadn't thrown his hard hat into the mix."

Plum shrugged. "So you two are in the same business. It gives you something in common."

I glanced at the now-cold pizza with its congealing cheese. Another slice of it would be preferable to the turn this conversation had taken.

"He's not my type." That much was true. He was as far away from being the type of man I wanted as Nashville was from Paris (the city in France, not the small Tennessee town a little over a hundred miles away).

"Shame." Plum stared across the room at Parker and then shrugged, apparently satisfied with my answer.

Hope, on the other hand, was not. "I don't get you at all. One minute you're looking like the only kid on the block with no ice cream, because everyone is paired off except you. The next, you're saying a man, who if you ask me is crazy about your rude behind, isn't your type."

Crazy about me? Huh? It was no secret that Hope was a lightweight when it came to alcohol. Clearly she had something else in her drink besides water.

"Nobody asked you. Besides, that's the stupidest thing I've heard all day."

Hope lifted a brow. "Maybe, but I saw the way he looked at you before you ran him off."

My sister was off her rocker. Parker viewed me the same way I saw him, as unfriendly competition. That's all. "I already told you, he isn't my type."

She pursed her lips. "Then how about telling us exactly what your type *is*?"

Plum leaned forward in her chair, awaiting my answer. They'd obviously thought the question would stump me, but I not only knew the type of man I wanted, I'd actually seen him, every morning for a few weeks now.

The waitress returned to our table and we all declined refills on our drinks. She eyed the pizza. "Want me to grab a to-go box?"

I shook my head, so she pulled a leather folio with the check from her uniform pocket and left it on the table. I glanced at it briefly to make sure it also included the tab for my crew. We won, so Sinclair Construction paid. If we lost, they could buy their own food and drinks. I tucked my company credit card in the folio and slid it to the edge of the table.

My sister and best friend's stares

remained fixed on me.

"Just what I thought," Hope said smugly. "She doesn't know her type at all. She's just being contrary, as usual."

Plum nodded in agreement. "Riley being Riley."

I should have just let it go, but the two of them were such know-it-alls. "My type doesn't wear a hard hat or steel-toe work boots." My words were soft and tentative as my mind conjured up the man I had watched stride in and out of the office building across the street from one of our job sites. I saw him twice a day: once during the morning rush when office workers descended downtown, and again at the end of the workday. "He wears a suit and tie."

Hope's chin hit her chest, while Plum motioned with her hand for me to continue, so I did.

"My type goes to work with a laptop bag slung over his shoulder, not a tool belt slung around his hips, and he looks like he just stepped off the cover of *GQ magazine*."

I continued to tell them what little I knew about the man who ruled my dreams. "He works with his brain, not his hands."

Plum and Hope continued to gawk at me, but I was unsure whether it was over the type of man I wanted, or the fact that I had a type in the first place.

Plum's eyes narrowed. "Sounds to me like this guy is more than a hypothetical type.

Have you met someone?"

I shook my head. Every time he walked past, I fantasized about him finally noticing me, but he was always on his phone. Besides, who would notice a woman in a hard hat and worn jeans, usually covered in grime or concrete dust?

"Well, this is a surprise," Hope said. "I never knew about this type of yours, or that you wanted someone so refined and…don't take this the wrong way, but the total opposite of you."

Neither had I, until I saw him. But it didn't matter. In fact, I felt ridiculous for even mentioning it. Nothing would ever come of my infatuation with a stranger.

"I just wanted to make it clear: Hudson Parker is not, and will never be, the man for me." My gaze drifted to the other side of the room, where he was standing at the bar talking to the guys. Suddenly, he looked over their heads and met my stare head-on. The scrutiny of his dark-eyed gaze sent another shiver through places on my body that shouldn't be responding to anything concerning him. I abruptly turned away and was relieved my dining companions were none the wiser.

Hope pulled out her phone and frowned at the screen. "I'd better get going."

I stifled a yawn with my fist. "Yeah, me too."

"Hold on, before everybody scatters, we're

still on for tomorrow night, right?" Plum asked.

"Of course! Do you actually think I'd miss *Hot Mess* after last week's cliff-hanger?" I asked. "I've got to see how Delilah is going to fix this latest mess she's gotten herself into."

Hot Mess was currently the number one show in the country; a true television phenomenon. Every Friday night eyeballs were glued to the screen to see what kind of trouble the series' main protagonist, Delilah Cole, portrayed by Golden Globe–nominee Nova Night, was going to get into. And more importantly, how she was going to get out of it.

Savvy and educated, as well as a style trendsetter, the character of Delilah was the perfect blend of beauty and moxie. Every week, the fictitious business consultant had her choice of the most powerful men in the country, and they all hung on her every word.

Add that scandalous family of hers to the mix, and things got very *messy*, as the show's title inferred.

"It's your turn to play host, Riley. You making pizza?" Plum smacked her lips. "I know we just had one tonight, but it doesn't compare to yours."

I wasn't much on the cooking front, but I made a helluva homemade pizza. Better than the one we'd just eaten, for sure.

"No can do. I won't have time." I made a

mental note to stop by Publix's deli on the way home to place an order for a ready-made tray. I could pick it up tomorrow after work. "You're bringing dessert, right?"

"Yep, cake pops. Your favorite," Plum replied.

I smiled. "Bring extra."

"Will do." She turned to my sister. "You have drinks covered, Hope?"

My sister looked up from her phone. "Count me out, guys. I won't be able to make it."

Plum fisted her hands on her hips. "What on earth do you have to do that's more important than watching *Hot Mess*?"

"Dinner with my fiancé's boss," Hope replied. "Rob just texted. It's apparently one of those you-had-better-be-there affairs."

"Oh, I almost forgot. Tammy and Candace aren't coming, either. Tammy's in-laws are in town, and Candace has a Lamaze class," Plum said.

It didn't come as a surprise. Once our single friends became half of a married couple, things changed. Sure, they always vowed our girls' night would go on as before, but despite their good intentions, their newfound marital obligations took priority.

Plum would do the same once she tied the knot on Christmas Eve next year. Hope hadn't even said, "I do" yet, but she'd already started.

Standing, I glanced around the

restaurant. Some of the guys had started to filter out, but there were players from both teams still watching the game. I didn't care as long as the ones who worked with me punched the clock on time tomorrow morning. "So do I need to order an entire platter or just a couple of sandwiches?"

"A small platter should do it," Plum said, gathering her things. "Tiffani, Ginger, and Alison are still coming."

Hope shook her head. "Nope, Alison has a big date at some fancy restaurant Saturday night. She took off work tomorrow to have a spa day, because she's expecting Derek to propose."

Girls' night was a big deal to me. I worked mostly with men, and the few women on my crew were mothers who spent their time off the job caring for their kids. They didn't have time for the company softball team or getting together after work.

I sighed as Hope continued to fill us in on Alison and Derek. With everyone coupling up, it wouldn't be long before our girls' night watching *Hot Mess* turned into girl night, and I ended up watching it solo. When that happened, I'd have to find a new favorite show, because the thought of sitting home alone watching Delilah Cole juggle her choice of good-looking men was just too damn depressing.

CHAPTER 2

HUDSON

The bartender's eyes sparkled with an unspoken invitation as she slid the drink in front of me. Her fingertips brushed my hand and lingered.

"Sure there isn't something else you'd like?" She leaned across the bar, close enough that I could hear the dulcet tones of her voice despite the boisterous conversations of the guys on either side of me watching the game on the big-screen televisions strategically placed around the sports bar. "How about something sweet?" she continued. "That still packs a punch?"

No doubt about it: the woman was hot. She rocked sexy curves that ebbed and flowed in all the right spots, and she had a pretty face that had lit up the moment I'd walked through the door. Running her tongue over her full bottom lip, she tugged at the hem of her cropped shirt until the name tag that read Julie was nearly at her navel. The V-neck revealed a black lace bra that barely contained a pair of surgically enhanced double Ds.

It was an invitation I might have taken her up on, but tonight I wasn't interested. My dick wasn't, either. "The beer will do for now, but thanks for the offer."

She shrugged. "Well, if you change your mind, I'm off the clock at ten."

The beautiful bartender didn't hold my attention any more than the game, or the guys from Mills Plumbing and Sinclair Construction who were talking about it. I turned away from the bar just in time to watch Atlanta's baseball team let the New York Mets walk away with a four-game sweep.

"The Braves ain't shit," Cal Webber bellowed.

A chorus of voices echoed his sentiment. Although the Braves were my team, I couldn't argue. It was the same old thing with them. I took a deep swig from my bottle of beer as the conversation turned to what the Braves could do to salvage their season. Usually, I would have been all in, but tonight my thoughts had been hijacked. It happened every single time I laid eyes on Riley Sinclair. I looked past the television to the table she shared with her sister and colorfully dressed friend.

I managed to nod and offer an interested-sounding *hmmm* to appear as if I was contributing to the discussion going on around me. However, Riley was the only person in the room who commanded my attention.

It didn't make sense. She wasn't the most beautiful woman I'd ever seen, and unlike Julie on the other side of the bar, Riley had nothing for me. Not even a smile. If our exchanges were any indication, the head of Sinclair Construction hated my guts.

The fact that we ran competing companies was part of it. Parker Construction had won a contract or two the Sinclairs had bid on, and it hadn't sat well with the oldest Sinclair sister. But what really stuck in Riley's craw were the two championship trophies that were once a fixture in her company's offices and now stood proudly in mine.

I didn't care nearly as much about them as she did, but my possession of them kept Riley up in my face, and I liked that, a lot. There was little chance of the erotic scenarios my imagination conjured up at the sight of her playing out in real life, though. A Popsicle had a better chance of surviving a hot oven beside a Thanksgiving turkey than I had of getting in Riley Sinclair's panties.

No matter, I thought. I wasn't a man who had to chase tail. Nor did I pine for a woman who didn't want me, even if I did find her sexy as hell.

So why are you here?

Because some of the guys had asked me to stop by, and my baby sister and her offspring had invaded my home. I was rationalizing. Deep down, I knew the real reason.

You knew she'd be here.

I continued to check Riley out on the sly.

A baseball cap with her team's emblem turned backward covered the tangle of sandy-brown dreadlocks that usually grazed her shoulders. I flashed back to earlier this evening at the park when she'd stomped up the bleacher stairs, that brazen confidence of hers on full display. I'd sat on my hands to keep from pulling the cap off her head and threading my fingers through those ropes of thick hair.

All I wanted was to haul her against me and kiss that brash mouth. I'd stared at her lips, a tempting shade of pink that hadn't come from a tube, as she gloated over Sinclair's win and promised my team an even worse trouncing if we met in the playoffs or championship game. I watched her now, smiling and laughing. She'd had no idea how close she'd come to being kissed so thoroughly the only word coming out of her mouth would have been my name, riding on her breathless sigh.

"So what's your take on it, Parker?"

I blinked at the sound of my surname and saw several expectant faces. "Huh?"

"Cal asked your opinion on the rumored Braves coaching changes." Owen Mills, whose team had suffered a loss at the hands of Riley's this evening, slapped me on the back. "Where's your head at, man?"

I shared my thoughts on the Braves, but left the latter question unanswered. It was time I finish my drink and be on my way.

Owen nudged me with an elbow. "That gorgeous bartender has been checking you out since you got here. She can't take her eyes off you," he said. "I know, because I've been checking her out all night."

I glanced toward the bar. Julie smiled seductively; it was obvious her earlier invitation was still open. Maybe I should take her up on it. A few hours with her would be just the thing to take my mind off...

"Damn, I thought she'd never leave." Deke Boyd, an outfielder from Sinclair Construction's team, guzzled his beer.

"Who?" Both Cal and I asked simultaneously.

"Our boss, of course," Deke replied to Cal. "Hard-ass Riley," he added for my benefit.

We all turned to the now-empty table across the room. After practically eye-fucking her all evening, I hadn't even seen her go. Good. If she was out of sight, maybe I could finally get her off my mind.

"Come on, man. I'll admit the last time she gave me a hearty slap on the back for doing a good job, my back hurt for a week," Cal said. "But Riley's all right."

"All right?" Deke asked incredulously.

"Did you see the way she chewed me out for missing that ball earlier?" He immediately launched into an imitation of Riley's voice. "Pull your head outta your ass and keep it in the game, Deke! My granny could have made that catch."

The spot-on rendition of his boss elicited laughter from most of the men standing around the television.

The second baseman from the Sinclair team joined in. "I struck out in the third inning, and the look she gave me nearly scorched my eyebrows off." He visibly shivered. "I thought she was gonna dock my pay."

"The woman does take the game seriously." Owen rubbed the stubble on his chin with the back of his hand.

Riley's genuine love of sports was another point in her favor as far as I was concerned. My ex-wife had been an avid sports fan. Well, she'd *pretended* to be until I put a ring on her finger. Two weeks after the honeymoon, the same woman who had cheered through games bitched every time I mentioned attending one or even turned on the sports channel.

"We're supposed to be having fun out there," Deke said. "But Riley acts like it's the World Series."

Cal took a sip of his beer. "Riley's good people, a good boss, and better than any man I've ever worked for in my twenty years in construction."

Deke opened his mouth to object, but Cal cut him off.

"When you fell off a ladder two years ago replacing the shingles on your roof after that tornado, who sat in the emergency room and waited with your son and ex-wife to make sure you were okay?"

Cal hit him with another question, not waiting for an answer to the first. "Who continued to pay your salary while you recovered from surgery, even though you weren't hurt on the job? *Riley*, that's who."

Deke held up his hands in surrender. "Okay, okay. As far as bosses go, she's better than most," he conceded with a grumble.

"I like working for her."

Hudson didn't recognize the guy who made the comment, but several of the men from Sinclair nodded in agreement. "But when it comes to the softball and bowling leagues, Riley's a beast," the same guy added.

"Only if you screw up," Cal clarified.

"Spoken like a man who managed to get a home run off Owen here." Deke said.

Owen grunted. "That was just a lucky hit."

"You boys should spend less time bitching and moaning and more time working on your game," Cal said. "Then the boss won't have to ride herd on you."

"Or perhaps," Deke took a deep swig from another brew. *"She needs somebody riding her.* Maybe it'll soften some of those rough edges of hers."

A mouthful of beer spewed from between Owen's lips, spraying the front of Deke's shirt. Two other guys nearly choked on their drinks.

"R-Riley?" Sinclair's second baseman stammered.

I'd stood mute for the majority of the conversation and had intended to remain that way, but my thoughts managed to bypass my internal censor. "There's nothing wrong with Riley or a few rough edges."

Owen shrugged. "I guess I don't think of her that way. I see her more as friend material. You know, one of the guys."

Grumbles of agreement echoed through our gathering. "Yeah, I just can't picture her as girlfriend material," someone else said.

"Unless the guy is a pro wrestler who fights MMA matches on the side," Deke said.

"Oh, come on. She's okay-looking," another voice chimed in.

"Would you ask her out?" Deke asked.

"Uh...nope," the same voice replied.

Another guy from Mills Plumbing spoke for the first time. "Me neither. I mean, she's kinda cute in a Riley kind of way, but the truth is, she's just too intimidating."

"What about you, Cal?" Deke asked.

"I'm married," he replied. "Besides, I want no part of that question."

"Suck up," Deke teased.

"Hey, nothing wrong with staying on the boss's good side," Cal said. "I've got a family to feed."

I drained the bottle of beer I'd been nursing since I'd walked through the door. It was past time I left. Cal had the right idea. This was a conversation I didn't want any part of. Even though I was firmly on the opposite of Riley Sinclair's good side, the topic hit too close to home.

"I'd better call it a night, fellas," I said. "Got an early morning."

"We all do," Cal concurred.

"What about you, Parker?" Deke called out.

I stopped and turned around. "What about me?"

"Couldn't help notice the way Riley nearly stripped the hide off you with that sharp tongue of hers at the park."

The second baseman chimed in. "Anybody else would have given it right back to her. Or even decked her, if she were a man. Instead, you looked amused."

"The woman's a little competitive," I shrugged. "Nothing wrong with that, or her."

"If I didn't know better, I'd think you'd do more than ask her out," Owen said.

"I've thought about it," I admitted. More than thought about it.

Deke snorted. "Man, your dick must have a death wish."

Leave it, I thought, but the words escaped

before I could catch them. "One night in my bed, and Riley Sinclair would be up the next morning cooking breakfast, wearing nothing but an apron, high heels and a satisfied smile."

CHAPTER 3

RILEY

Like a song you can't get out of your head, Hudson Parker's words replayed in my head the next day at work. I'd been halfway home last night when I couldn't remember getting my company credit card back from the waitress. I'd checked my wallet at the next stoplight, and sure enough, the slot I'd kept it in was empty. Making a quick U-turn, I'd returned to the sports bar.

About the same time I discovered my credit card in my back pocket, the sound of familiar male voices filtered out to the small lobby. It was obvious they were talking about me. I chalked it up to beer talk. None of them would have the nerve to say any of it to my face.

Who cared what they thought, anyway? As I'd admitted to Hope and Plum earlier, none of them were my type. As long as they gave me a good day's work and kept their opinions to themselves, we'd continue to get along just fine. Then Parker's outlandish declaration hit me right between the eyes.

...wearing nothing but an apron, high heels and a satisfied smile.

Not only was the man an ass, he was a delusional one. I grunted as I stood in the midst of one of our current sites, the renovation of the Espresso Cosmetics building. Ignoring the scaffolding, dust and debris, I continued to examine the subcontractors' work to make sure everything was on track to complete this project on time.

Yet my thoughts continued to drift toward Parker. Why had I slipped out of the sports bar instead of letting him know I'd overheard him and given him a piece of my mind?

The truth was that his words had had the effect of a zap from a stun gun. They'd briefly paralyzed me and left me utterly speechless.

"I'd rather sleep with the devil," I muttered under my breath. *Then why did you dream about doing a lot more than just sleeping with him last night?*

I shrugged off the silent question that was as ridiculous as Hudson Parker thinking he could put me in a dick coma and magically transform me into a sex-drunk, bacon-frying zombie.

Besides, the workday was winding down. It was payday Friday. Bad enough that the man was a pain in my company's backside. I didn't intend to waste any more brain cells thinking about Parker. Or spend another night dreaming about him, *naked*.

"You satisfied?" My project manager, Cal Webber, who'd been standing beside me, roused me out of my wandering thoughts.

Cal and I had worked together for years, and these were calls I trusted him to make. The massive renovation of the skyscraper that housed Espresso Cosmetics headquarters was more than just another job, however, and not just because my cousin was Espresso's CEO. My dad had erected this very building back in 1980, when he ran Sinclair Construction. It was important for me to improve upon his work and modernize the structure for generations to come.

"Everything looks good," I said finally. "Great actually."

"If it didn't, we wouldn't be working with these subcontractors," he replied.

My internal alarm sounded. This wasn't the same as the one that woke me up before dawn on weekday mornings for a three-mile run. It was the twice-a-day silent signal that my mystery crush, who I'd nearly told my friend and sister about last night, would be exiting the building across the street and walking past the Espresso building.

I didn't know what I'd do once we'd completed this project and more of my attention was needed at the new subdivision we'd broke ground on north of downtown. Until then, I was just going to enjoy glimpses of the hunk in a suit who ticked every box on my checklist of what I wanted in a man.

Seeing him again was sure to get Parker off my mind. Deep down, though, I knew I had a better chance of getting struck by lightning than my mystery man noticing I was alive.

Plum and Hope wouldn't believe their eyes if they could see me now. Standing at the temporary fence we'd erected around the building site, I stared through the chain links at the business offices across the street. My breath caught each time the door opened, only to release when the person exiting wasn't him.

I'd stalked...er, seen him go in this morning. He never reappeared at lunch when the other downtown worker drones filed out of the surrounding buildings to forage for food. Probably too busy taking care of important business, or possibly even running one, I reasoned, though I had nothing to back up my speculation. Just a gut feeling the aura of power surrounding him seemed to suggest. The man carried himself like a boss.

The door swung open again, and the breath I'd been holding morphed into a dreamy sigh as he walked out onto the sidewalk. His navy suit and pale-blue shirt were as crisp as they'd been this morning.

His tie, loosened at the neck, was the only indication he was at the end of his workday. A leather messenger bag was slung over one shoulder, and the ever-present earbuds connected to his cell phone were jammed in his ears.

I greedily sucked in the sight of him before his long stride could eat up the street in front of me. My eyes did what my hands couldn't. In my imagination, my palm caressed the caramel skin of his clean-shaven face, and my fingers smoothed his close-cropped hair. Then I touched the pad of my thumb to his bottom lip to gauge if it was as soft and kissable as it looked.

I gawked at his mouth as he talked animatedly into the earbud's small microphone. I couldn't hear him through all the noise from our site as well as other construction sites in the city's revitalized downtown, but whoever was on the other line was definitely rubbing him the wrong way.

Then all too soon, he was gone.

My fingers clutched the chain-link fence. Once we wrapped up this project, I'd probably never see him again unless he finally noticed me, or I finally summoned the guts to take charge of the situation, like I did every other one in my life.

Just introduce yourself and ask him out.

Sure, Riley. Why don't you do that, I thought.

There were at least a dozen reasons why it

was a terrible idea. I hadn't spied a gold band on his finger, but that didn't mean he wasn't married or wrapped up in a relationship with someone special. Even if the man was free, the women in his life were more than likely the antithesis of me, with sleek bodies they spent hours honing with Pilates and barre classes when they weren't busy working as brain surgeons or doing world-saving volunteer work.

Long story short, the guy was out of my league.

My body was more sturdy than sleek, and I had unmanageable dreads that had undoubtedly frizzed beneath my hard hat, but all of this still didn't keep a blue-collar woman from hoping.

I glanced down at my work boots and then resumed staring across the street at the sidewalk he'd walked along. Too bad I wasn't more like Delilah Cole. The Hot Mess heroine would have marched right across the street and talked to him. Then again, Delilah didn't have to approach a man. They usually came to her, in droves.

The guys working on the Espresso building began to file past me. It was quitting time on payday Friday. Nobody would linger long.

"What are you thinking about so hard?" Cal asked, his now-empty lunch box in hand.

"A lost cause," I mumbled, pushing off the fence.

He gave me a brief, quizzical look before shaking off my strange reply. "Doing anything this weekend?"

I shrugged. "Watching television with some friends tonight, but that's about it."

"Hot Mess?" He raised a brow.

"Yeah, it's our favorite show."

Cal chuckled. "It's everybody's favorite show," he said. "Delilah Cole." He shook his head. "Umph, umph, umph."

"So you're a fan?" I asked, grateful to be thinking about something besides a man I didn't want to want and another who more than likely would never want me.

"Don't get me wrong. I love my wife," Cal said. "But Delilah Cole is must-see TV."

CHAPTER 4

HUDSON

My work wife barged into my office wearing an expression that made me glad I no longer had a real one.

Ignoring the interruption, along with the huffing sound she made as she folded her arms over her chest, I returned my attention to the interview I was conducting with the young man seated on the other side of my desk. "Please continue. I believe you were telling me about your work experience."

The kid shrugged. "This would be my first job, so I don't have any. Your posting in the student athletic center said it wasn't necessary," he added hurriedly. "Plus, your company's paying way more than the minimum wage summer jobs around campus."

I nodded and gave the application he'd handed me earlier a cursory glance. "We're willing to take extracurricular activities into consideration, and it says here you're on the baseball team." I tried to sound casual. "Did I mention we also have a company softball team?"

A grunt erupted from the other side of the room. "Bet it was the first thing you mentioned."

The young man squirmed in his seat. He looked from me to the business-suit-clad woman standing in the corner, frowning and tapping her foot. Unofficially, I referred to her as my work wife because we worked together so closely. Her official title, however, was vice president of Parker Construction.

The Fisk University alumnus was not only smart and savvy; her presence in the office insured I wasn't stuck behind my desk all day. I could be on-site, keeping an eye on the company's various projects all over town, and doing the hands-on work I loved.

Still, when the business end of the company required my personal attention, as it had in my earlier meetings, I suited up and took care of it.

The interviewee rattled off his baseball stats with the college team, as well as his willingness to join our company softball team if he was hired.

Winding up the interview, I shook his extended hand and told him someone from my office would be in touch. "On your way out, please tell my receptionist I'm ready for the next candidate."

The young man opened his mouth to agree, but Alicia cut him off. "Never mind. I'll do it," she said. "I want to talk with Mr. Parker first."

She closed the door behind him and focused on me. "Mind explaining why our outer offices are filled with college students in baseball and softball uniforms?"

"If you have to ask, maybe you aren't as bright as I give you credit for."

"Ha, ha. You're hilarious," she deadpanned.

Loosening my tie's grip on my neck, I leaned back in the leather executive chair behind the battered metal desk I'd bought used from Goodwill years ago, back when I operated the business out of a trailer in Atlanta. Alicia plopped down in the seat across from me and toed off her pumps.

"I can't believe you're hiring ringers so you can hold on to that stupid statue for another year."

She spared a glance at the credenza on the other side of the room bearing both a first place bowling league trophy in the shape of a crystal bowling pin, and a two-foot column trophy topped with a gleaming gold softball. A spotlight I'd had installed shone down on both of them. The one in question proclaimed Parker Construction last year's champions of the Music City Blue-Collar Intramural

Softball League.

"That's more than a mere statue. It's a year's worth of bragging rights."

"Your having it also annoys the hell out of Riley Sinclair," she said.

The mention of the woman's name roused images I'd tried to put out of my mind while tossing and turning last night. Not that they'd ever come to fruition. Riley couldn't stand me.

"I guess she's still adjusting to the fact that the trophy has a new home. Until we won last year, both of them had been in Sinclair Construction's hands for years."

Alicia's prematurely silver hair swished from side to side as she shook her head and laughed. "I don't know why the two of you don't screw each other's brains out and get it out of your systems."

"W-what?" I sputtered. "Where did that come from?"

"Everyone else might be blind to it, but I've seen what happens when you two are in the same room."

"Yeah, Riley blows up or tries to goad me."

Alicia raised a brow. "Or you find a way to press her buttons."

I grunted. "The mere sight of me presses Riley's buttons."

A knowing smile tugged at the corners of my vice president's lips. "Oh, I'll just bet it does."

Rubbing the back of my neck, I shook my

head. “But not in the way you’re thinking.”

“Oh, it’s exactly in the way I’m thinking.”

Alicia’s intuition was usually spot-on. Too bad this time she couldn’t be more wrong. “Then you’re mistaken. I saw Riley twice yesterday. The first time she told me in no uncertain terms she was coming for that trophy after her team wiped the floor with ours. Later, the woman nearly staged a revolt at the thought of my sitting at the same table over at First Down.”

Alicia’s soft laughter filled the office as my mobile phone lit up with an incoming call. I stared at my younger sister’s name and number scrolling across the small screen for a long moment, before turning the phone face down unanswered. Caryn was grown, and a lifetime of being spoiled by the men in her life had done her more harm than good. Still, old habits were hard to break.

I returned my attention to Alicia. “Your theory doesn’t hold up,” I continued. “If she could, Riley would push my face into the baseball diamond and make me eat dirt.”

It was a catch-22. The woman’s independence, drive and competitive nature topped the qualities I found so damned attractive about her. On the flip side, they’d also made her view me as the enemy.

“Exactly.” Alicia’s eyes sparkled, and her smile morphed into a full-fledged smirk.

“I’m not following you.”

“Riley is like the little tomboy on the

playground. She won't come right out and tell the boy she's hung up on how she feels, but she never misses an opportunity to get in his face, either. Don't forget, I've been in the same room as you two. When she thinks you're not looking, she can't take her eyes off you."

Really. My face remained impassive, but inside I was grinning like a fool.

"And this softball business." She waved a hand in the direction of the trophies. "Come on, Parker." She lifted a brow. "Is it the championship you really want? Or are the ringers and everything else just excuses to keep Riley coming for you?"

The question hung in the air. We both knew the answer.

Alicia shook her head and laughed in the way adults do at a toddler's antics. "You two are ridiculous."

While deep down I knew it was just one person's opinion, and that this could be the rare time Alicia was wrong, part of me couldn't help but get a kick out of the idea that Riley might be feeling me as much as I felt her. Maybe it was time for me to let that sassy, stubborn construction diva know I wanted to sex the hell out of her.

Clearing her throat, Alicia rose from her chair. "If you don't need me for anything else, I'm going to clear out of here. I want to have the kids fed and in bed by the time *Hot Mess* comes on."

"Hot...what?"

"Come on, Hudson. Don't tell me you don't know about *Hot Mess*?"

"No clue."

"It's only the number one television show in the country!"

"I only watch three things on television—baseball, basketball, and football."

"What do you do when the seasons are over?"

"I curl into a ball and cry myself to sleep until they return."

Alicia rolled her eyes. "I'll send in your next intern...I mean, ringer candidate on my way out."

Her skirt caught on the edge of my metal desk as she turned to go. "Dang it!" She looked down at the tear and groaned. "This was brand new, and the only skirt in my closet I hadn't snagged on that raggedy desk of yours."

"Buy some new ones and put it on your expense account," I said absently.

"What I need to do is order you a new desk and get rid of that thing," she grumbled.

Alicia walked out of my office, but her wardrobe malfunction was the furthest thing from my mind. All I could think about was what she'd said earlier. *Why don't you and Riley Sinclair just screw each other's brains out and get it out of your systems?*

CHAPTER 5

RILEY

So much for girls' night.

I put my phone on speaker and listened as another friend made her excuses for not being able to make it. They all sounded the same to me. *Blah, blah, I can't... Blah, blah, my man this, and blah, blah, my man that...*

You'd think the men in their lives had sugar on their sticks, because none of my friends seemed to be able to tear themselves away from them. Not even for an evening.

"No problem, Ginger," I told her. "Next week, then."

Ending the call, I looked at the platter of sandwich fixings and wine I'd put out in anticipation of their arrival. I wasn't sure if I was missing my girls or envious of them. I honestly couldn't remember the last time I'd had some sugar stick, or even an offer of one.

Hope's asinine idea that Hudson Parker

had the hots for me popped into my head, along with a slow-motion memory of his backside in those low-slung jeans as he walked away from our table last night. I blinked it away.

Okay, I could concede the man's ass had a certain appeal, but that was it. The only thing I wanted from Parker was the safe delivery of the softball and bowling trophies back into Sinclair hands once we won then back.

Grabbing the remote, I turned on the television and started making myself a sandwich from the fixings on the platter. Plum could make her own when she got here with dessert, seeing as it would just be me and her tonight. I was slathering mustard on a slice of rye bread when my phone rang.

Sighing, I glanced down at the small touch screen and rolled my eyes. "Plum Watson, you'd better not be calling to say you're canceling, too," I barked into the phone. "I've been looking forward to red velvet cake pops all day."

"It's Doug, hon," she said.

"Not you, too! Don't bother explaining. I've been getting calls from dick-whipped women all night saying they can't make it."

"No. I'm in the emergency room with him," Plum said.

I immediately switched from annoyed friend mode and began searching for my car keys. "Oh, my God, which hospital? I'll come right over."

"No need. Doctor says he broke his arm."

"You sure?"

"Yeah, stay home and watch the show. I'm going to watch on the waiting room television while they finish treating him," Plum said. "In fact, the show's about to start. Talk to you later."

Girls' night canceled, I moved operations to my bedroom, switched on the TV and poured wine into a goblet that was bigger than my head. Being single wasn't so bad, I thought, mentally counting off the perks. I came and went as I pleased without reporting to anyone. I could drink wine and eat in bed if I wanted. And last but not least, battery-operated boyfriends didn't complain or judge.

Then again, if the right man shared my queen-size bed, food and wine would be the last thing on my mind. As I donned my pj's, my imagination conjured up images of my crush shedding his designer business suit and climbing into my bed. I'd probably melt into a puddle of goo if that particular fantasy ever came true.

"Good Lawd." I took a gulp of wine to wet my suddenly parched throat.

The intro music to *Hot Mess* started up in the background, rousing me from my illicit revelry. I dived onto the bed and cranked up the volume on the remote. Forgoing my sandwich, I reached for the long-stemmed glass and took a healthy sip from it.

Delilah Cole filled my television screen. She was wearing a slinky red bandage dress, and right away my phone started chirping with notifications. I ignored it. Although my Twitter feed was always hilarious during *Hot Mess*, it could also be distracting, and I wanted to focus on my weekly guilty pleasure and enjoy my wine.

Minutes later, I stared incredulously at the screen. "Look at this heiffa. Agreed to two dates in one night, and I haven't had one in..." I paused to think. "Oh, hell. I can't even remember."

The fact that this was a television show didn't stop me from being jealous.

After going out for coffee with a delicious-looking hunk who appeared to be a good ten years younger than Delilah's thirty-two, she moved on to a late dinner with the older gentleman she'd been dating all season.

The two of them dined at a posh French restaurant and returned to her place. I estimated her dinner date to be in his mid-to-late forties. Still, he was both fit and fine. The strands of silver overtaking his short-cropped hair only added to his aura of power and masculine appeal. Like her, both of Delilah's dates were entrepreneurs. One wore jeans and two-hundred-dollar sneakers, while the other stuck with expensive Italian suits.

I drained my wineglass and scrambled

into the kitchen for a refill during the commercial break. Thirty minutes into the hour-long show, Delilah emerged from her bedroom in a sexy satin nightie only to find the older man asleep on the sofa.

She nudged him. The only response was his snores filling the living room of her stylish Boston town house.

"Damn." An obviously sexually frustrated Delilah delivered the sexy pout that had become her trademark to the viewing audience. Her doorbell rang, and her sleeping date settled deeper into the sofa.

Delilah flung open the door to find the guy she'd had coffee with earlier on the other side of it. Both her gaze and the camera zeroed in on the younger man's devastating smile before panning out to the wicked gleam in his dark bedroom eyes. A burgundy T-shirt fit his hard body so well that I barely noticed he was bearing a single red rose.

Goodness, he was fine. I took another sip of wine.

The show cut to commercial, and the chimes of text messages and Twitter notifications blew up my phone. I grabbed it, intending to silence the noise, when it suddenly rang in my palm.

"Oh, my God. Did you see him standing at her door looking good enough to eat?" Plum asked, without preamble. "What do you think she's going to do?"

I shrugged. "Take the rose and send him

home. I mean, what can she do? That silver fox is asleep on her couch."

"You're probably right," Plum sighed into the phone. "But did you see the way his body filled her doorway? He's so tall...and the breadth of his shoulders... I know what *I'd* do."

"You wouldn't." Then I remembered the reason why we weren't watching the show together. "How's Doug?"

"They just released him."

"Then why aren't you on the way home?"

"You're kidding, right?" Plum sucked her teeth. "We aren't going anywhere. We're going to sit right here in this waiting room until *Hot Mess* is over."

"Plum," I admonished.

"They gave him a pain shot," she said. "He's fine."

A commercial for long-wear lipstick ended, and once again, Delilah and her handsome, unexpected guest dominated the screen.

"Gotta go!" Plum ended the call just as our favorite TV heroine grabbed the younger man by the waistband of his jeans and pulled him inside her town house. He wasted no time in laying a kiss on Delilah; it was so hot I could feel the heat through my television. The rose in his hand fell to the gleaming hardwood floor in slow motion, and they continued to kiss as if nothing else mattered.

When they finally came up for air, the young stud looked over Delilah's shoulder at his competition, still asleep on the couch. "What's up with your dad?"

Delilah smirked, and I laughed out loud. "You know good and well he's not my father, and he's not that old. Don't you recognize one of the most powerful businessmen in New England when you see him?"

"Not when there's drool on the side of his face," the younger man quipped. "So are you going to wake up Pops and send him back to the nursing home, or should I go?"

Delilah cocked a perfectly arched brow. A smile played on her full lips. "Neither."

He met her smile with one of his own, signaling he'd received her silent implication loud and clear. "Bedroom?"

"Can't wait that long." Delilah inclined her head toward the kitchen.

"Oh, Delilah." I shook my head at the television. "Girl, you really are a hot mess!"

I reached for my wine. The younger man on the screen reached for Delilah. She wrapped her long, gravity-defying legs around his waist as he carried her into the kitchen, kissing her the entire way. He pinned her against the only wall in the room free of stainless steel appliances before breaking the kiss. His eyes lit up as he cupped her bottom in his hands. "No panties?" he asked.

"Never bother with 'em," Delilah confirmed.

The two went at it against the wall. They

were in the midst of a second round on the granite countertop of the kitchen island bar when the camera cut to the older man on the sofa. *His phone was ringing.*

I drank deeply from my wineglass during the commercial break, wondering how Delilah was going to get out of this mess. How did one explain screwing one man while on a date with another? *Who does that?*

Hoisting my glass toward the television, I gave her a mock salute. “I’m not mad at ya, girl.”

The show ended with Delilah awaking to breakfast in bed, courtesy of the silver fox. “I hope you’ll forgive me for falling asleep after we got back from dinner,” he said. “I can’t believe I slept until morning.” He handed her a mug of coffee. “Hope you weren’t too lonely.”

She smiled at him as she applied a liberal smear of jam to a croissant. The camera didn’t miss the mischievous glint in her eye. “Not at all. It turned out to be a *very satisfying* evening.”

My eyes remained glued to the screen, eagerly awaiting previews for next week’s episode. If it was anything like this week’s show, it wouldn’t disappoint. Instead, another commercial aired.

“What the...”

I reached for the remote. My finger hovered over the off button, but the announcer’s spiel stopped me.

"Look like Delilah. Shop like Delilah. Be like Delilah. Learn how to land the man of your dreams, just like America's favorite television character, Delilah Cole."

Maybe it was all the wine I'd consumed, but the smooth voice definitely had my attention. Dammit, I wanted to land the man of my dreams.

"Then pick up your phone and download the official Delilah Cole app." The announcer spoke as if he could actually hear me. "It's ten bucks to download. After that, you'll pay only five dollars a month for tips that will help make you feel just like the most desirable woman on television."

Dropping the remote, I picked up my mobile phone and did a quick search for the app. I stared at the icon, a sultry picture of Delilah Cole, as I read the features aloud.

"How to get Delilah's style. Shopping tips, fashion and beauty tutorials. Delilah's favorite products." I closed my eyes briefly. My common sense warned me that this so-called app's true goal was to separate me from my hard-earned money. "You know better, Riley," I whispered.

Then I read the most important feature of all. "Use Delilah's advice to help you win the heart of any man you choose."

I thought about the man I wanted, the one that walked past me every day. Then I tapped my screen with my forefinger and watched the app begin to download.

The next morning, I awoke to the sound of pounding on my front door, accompanied by the relentless buzz of the doorbell. Both exacerbated the bongo-drum beat of my headache, the aftereffect of too much wine and too little food the night before.

Bam. Bam. Bam. Buzzzzz.

Go away. I pulled the covers over my head, and silently pleaded with whoever was at the door to stop.

"Come on, Riley, open up."

Plum. She continued to pummel the door like she had a beef with it. "I know you're in there," she yelled.

I swung open the door just as she'd raised her fist to give it another pounding. "Why are you beating on my door like a lunatic? I could have been out for a walk or something."

My friend smirked as she walked past me into the front room of my ranch-style house. "Your truck is parked in the driveway," she said. "Besides, this is the South. Nobody walks anywhere."

I picked up my phone, which I'd left on an end table, and noted the time. "Is there a reason why you're practically kicking in my door at seven o'clock on a Saturday morning?" I asked. "Shouldn't you be tending to your fiancé?"

Plum waltzed into my kitchen and began making coffee. "His mama came over to coddle him, so he'll be fine." She stopped measuring coffee grounds in a paper filter, looked at me, and frowned. "Well, what are you waiting for? Get dressed. I booked an appointment online: you're going to meet with a personal shopper in a hour, and then there's hair, a facial, makeup..."

"Huh?" Fisting a hand on one hip, I stared at my friend. "What in the hell are you talking about?"

Plum huffed out a sigh. "I'm talking about *Operation Delilah*."

"Come again?"

Shaking her head, she snatched the phone from my hand. She swiped and held it up to my face. The Delilah Cole app was open on the screen. Plum jabbed it, and a video clip began to play.

"Congratulations on downloading the official Delilah Cole app. You are on your way to having both the life—and man—of your dreams. First, we're going to work on your look."

Hazy details of the previous night came into focus. Watching *Hot Mess* alone in bed, after everyone had canceled on me to be with their men. Overdoing it with the wine. And finally, impulsively ordering this stupid app.

"But how did you know I downloaded it?"

Plum rounded the breakfast bar and resumed making coffee. "We talked last night after I got home from the emergency room, and you went on and on about how this app was going to finally help you snag you the man of your dreams."

She switched on the coffeemaker and turned to face me. Leaning against the counter, she folded her arms over her chest. "A man I thought was a figment of your imagination until you 'fessed up to gawking at him from afar."

She paused at the surprised expression on my face.

"You don't remember, do you?"

I shook my head and made a mental note to pour the remaining two bottles of wine on the tabletop down the drain. I rarely drank as much as I did last night. Apparently, I'd been a tipsy blabbermouth.

The fact that I'd been harboring a secret crush on a stranger for weeks was no longer a secret. Now that the morning light had lifted my wine fog, the app no longer seemed like the great idea it had been during my solo pity party.

"Okay, so there's this guy..." My voice trailed off as I searched for a word to describe him. After all, we hadn't met, and it seemed ludicrous for a grown-ass woman to be talking about a crush. "Anyway, this whole app idea is just plain dumb. I'm going to take the thing off my phone right this minute."

I reached for it, but Plum was quicker.

"Oh, no you don't!" She snatched the phone off the counter.

"Forget about what I said last night. I was talking out of my head."

Plum stuck my phone in her skirt pocket. "You still want this Adonis in a business suit you told me about?"

"Well, yeah, but..."

She cut me off. "So are you planning to approach him the next time you see him and introduce yourself?"

"Uh...I..." Every day I told myself I was going to do just that, but I never did.

"And how's the admire-him-from-afar thing working for you?"

"It's not." I finally managed to answer one of her questions.

"And won't Sinclair Construction be done with the Espresso building soon?"

Already knowing the answer to that question, she bulldozed on. "So that doesn't give you much time. Like you said last night, this app gives you a plan of action. You've got nothing to lose by giving it a shot."

"Nothing but ten dollars up front, and then five dollars a month," I grumbled.

Plum filled a mug with coffee and shoved it into my hands. "Get dressed. It's time to put *Operation Delilah* into play."

Two hours later, I stood in front of a three-way mirror in the dressing room of a department store recommended by the app, flanked by Plum and a personal shopper. The ensemble I wore was one of a dozen I'd tried on this morning.

"I don't know." The personal shopper, an older woman wearing a pencil skirt and a navy blazer, frowned. Her green eyes studied me over the rim of her glasses. "This outfit is exactly what Delilah Cole would wear, and the colors are perfect for you." She pursed her lips. "Still, something about it isn't quite right."

I wiggled uncomfortably in the skinny jeans that were cutting off my circulation, and pulled the clingy, revealing top over my exposed cleavage.

"It's not the outfit," Plum chimed in.

In the mirror, I saw her approach me from behind. She knocked away the hand covering my breasts and yanked the hem of the baby-blue top downward, deepening its V-neck, which already left nothing to the imagination.

"Plum!" I yelped.

"That's better," my friend replied.

The personal shopper consulted the app on my phone and snapped her fingers. "I forgot the push-up bra."

I glanced down at what I was already serving up in my standard bra. *Oh, hell no.* Before I could get a word out, the blazer-clad woman returned to the dressing room with a leopard-print padded bra dangling from her finger.

"The app recommends our Big Guns model

with extra lift," she said. "It comes with a matching Kiss My Cheeks thong panty, but I didn't bring it. Apparently, Delilah thinks panties are a waste of time."

Plum snatched the padded bra and shoved me into the dressing room again. "Put it on."

Exhaling, I did as I was told. How much worse could it be?

Turns out, *a lot* worse.

"My boobs look like basketballs," I protested, looking at my reflection in the three-way mirror. "I can practically rest my chin on them!"

The personal shopper nodded her head in approval. "Much better. Delilah Cole certainly knows her stuff," she said. "I'm putting that app on my phone tonight. Give my old man something to stick his face in besides sports on television and his plate at the dinner table."

Glancing at Plum, I hoped my friend would be the voice of reason, but I should've known better.

She beamed at me. "You look freaking hot, Riley, and we haven't even got to overhauling your hair and makeup yet."

My hand automatically went to my shoulder-length locs, and I spared my reflection another glance. "There's no way I'm wearing this in public." I shook my head. "Nope. I don't care what that app says."

Plum planted a fist on the hip of her tie-dyed skirt. "You want to catch the eye of that suit you've got it bad for?"

I nodded.

"Believe me, hon. The sight of you in this outfit will not only get his attention, it'll leave the man drooling."

I sighed and studied my reflection again. "I look like a hoochie."

"You look like a woman," Plum corrected.

The personal shopper returned with a selection of pastel dresses in her arms. She pinned me with her gaze. "Well, you certainly aren't going to attract that man wearing what you came in here with."

I stared longingly at my worn, paint-spattered jeans, faded Titans shirt, and standard-issue bra draped across the chair, before once again turning to the Riley in the mirror. "Do y'all really think so?"

"Delilah thinks so, and from the looks of you now, she obviously knows what she's talking about." Plum grabbed one of the dresses from the personal shopper and shoved it toward me. "Try this on next."

The moment I shed the tight jeans and top and slipped the flimsy pink garment over my head, I knew it was all wrong for me. I glanced down at the skirt of the dress and rolled my eyes. "For goodness sake, Delilah," I whispered. "What have you gotten me into?"

A hand holding a pair of high-heel sandals appeared over the top of the dressing room door. "The app also recommends these shoes.

Apparently Delilah's wearing them on next week's show."

"And get a move on," Plum bellowed. "You have an appointment for the works at Espresso Sanctuary Spa, and they certainly have a full afternoon of work ahead of them."

And folks called me rude, I thought, stumbling out of the small dressing room as I tried to balance on the impossibly high heels.

The personal shopper gasped. "What a difference the right dress makes!" She clasped her hands together, as if she were congratulating herself on the choice. "That app was right about pastels being softer on the eyes. You look amazing, young lady."

Plum let out a dreamy sigh. "It's gorgeous."

I looked in the mirror for confirmation and frowned. "Did it escape your attention that the hem on this thing is crooked? And it's see through!" Not to mention the fact that Delilah apparently eschewed panties. "There's no way I'm going *anywhere* bare-assed in a peekaboo dress."

"First of all, it's not crooked, dear," the personal shopper said. "It's an asymmetrical, hanky hemline." She spoke loudly and slowly, as if I were a child. Then she raised the above-the-knee skirt of the dress. "You can't actually see through it, either. There's a sheer mesh lining. So it's ultra feminine with just the right hint of sexy."

Snorting, I gave my two helpers the stink-eye. "Hello? I work in construction. Feminine dresses and forklifts don't mix."

The personal shopper tapped her finger against her lips. "Well, I might have a solution for that, too," she said tentatively. "A few months ago, I read an article in *Vogue* about an online boutique that caters to blue-collar women," she said. "They even sell pink hard hats."

"You have got to be freaking kidding me!" I sucked my teeth at the absurdity of showing up to a site in a pink hard hat.

Plum looked up the store's website on my phone. "Wow, they've got cute stuff and overnight delivery."

"The store was founded by a beauty-pageant-queen-turned-welder who was tired of going to men's stores hoping they had a women's section, or making do wearing clothes designed for men," the personal shopper said.

That I could relate to, but I'd been grabbing my work gear from a men's store for so long that I really hadn't thought about it. The tradeswomen I worked with ran into the same problem.

"Oh, my God!" Plum squealed. "They even sell pink work boots. Adorable!"

A grunt pushed past my lips. "Why don't I skip to work with a Barbie lunch box and pink ribbons in my hair? My crew's reaction would be the same. Not only would I be the butt of jokes, I'd never hear the end of it."

My sarcasm and concerns were brushed aside.

"Give me a break, Riley. Most of the men you work with are too damned intimidated by you to risk getting on your bad side," Plum said. "Plus, you're the boss, which means you can wear whatever you want."

The personal shopper nodded in agreement, as if she actually had a say in the matter.

"But what..." I began.

Plum interrupted my objection with a question of her own. "What about when Mr. Perfect asks you out on a date?"

An actual date with my not-so-secret crush? I hadn't dared to think or hope that far ahead.

Plum held up my phone. Instead of pink boots, Delilah's face filled the small screen as a video clip from the app began to play. "Every woman needs a get 'em-girl dress in her wardrobe arsenal," the TV vixen said. "One guaranteed to make a man's eyes pop out of his head."

As Delilah spoke, I imagined walking into an upscale restaurant to meet him, and his eyes lighting up at the sight of me. He'd even put away his ever-present phone. From there, my fantasies fast-forwarded to being on his arm on a classy date at the opera or the ballet. Not that I'd ever seen or had an interest in either.

I spun around in the mirror, and the filmy

skirt of the dress lifted and swished against my thighs. "I'll take it."

"Smart move," Plum said. "Now try on the rest of these."

She glanced at the clock on the wall as I took the pile of clothes she dumped into my arms. "And be quick about it," she said. "You've got hair appointments, a deep-cleansing facial, and a manicure and pedicure coming up in a little over an hour. And don't forget the makeup lesson and brow, lip, and Brazilian wax."

My chin dropped to my boobs, which thanks to my new Big Guns bra, wasn't much of a drop. "A Brazilian *what*?"

CHAPTER 6

RILEY

Plum nudged my arm with her elbow as she steered her yellow Volkswagen Beetle out of Espresso Sanctuary's parking lot late that afternoon. This was not a modern-day Beetle: it didn't benefit from the advances that had been made in car suspension over the decades. Nope, hers was a 1978 clunker. She referred to it as vintage, but its occupants felt a jarring shock if it rolled over so much as a pebble.

The last thing I needed at this moment.

"You still not talking to me?" Plum asked.

"Don't you dare say a word." I winced from the passenger seat as the vibration of my own voice shot straight to my crotch.

"Come on, Riley. How was I supposed to know this was your first time getting a Brazilian wax?"

"Because I told you so, that's why. I can't

believe I let you talk me into that…" I paused to search for a phrase to describe it. *"Spread-eagle torture."*

Plum shrugged. "Not me. The app."

I almost rolled my eyes, but thought better of it. I didn't want to aggravate the red, stinging spots where any excess eyebrow and fine upper lip hair had been ripped off my face by the root.

"Don't mention that app or Delilah Cole to me right now." I spoke softly, not wanting to aggravate the *other* tender spot where my hair had been eliminated by the root. "If I weren't in so much pain, I'd kick both of your behinds."

Plum smiled indulgently at my threat. "Okay, so you're a bit uncomfortable right now, but you look great. Your new hair color is amazing, and once the swelling goes down around your eyebrows, you'll be able to appreciate the light touch of Espresso's makeup artist."

I grunted in reply. After spending the entire day shopping and getting the works at the spa, I wasn't just sore: I was exhausted. I flipped on the radio, hoping it would take my mind off my misery.

A newscaster's voice came through the car's ancient speakers accompanied by bursts of static. "The downtown area continues to be plagued by a gang of muggers preying on workers headed home for the day. This week alone, two women and three men were robbed in separate incidents. All suffered minor injuries and were treated and released from Nashville General Hospital. The police chief has designated more officers to…"

Static muffled the rest of the story on the AM radio station, so Plum shut it off.

"You're working on two big downtown projects," she said. "Anybody from your crews robbed?"

I shook my head and grimaced. "From what I've heard, the victims have all been white-collar workers. I guess the muggers figure people in business suits are easier targets and will have more cash and valuables."

The car hit another bump in the road. "Ow! Ow! Ow!"

Plum sighed. "I can feel you giving me the stink-eye. But maybe you should think of your temporary discomfort as an investment in your future pleasure. After all, no guy wants to go down on Buckwheat's…"

I cut her off. "Don't you dare make me laugh."

She gave me an apologetic glance. "Sorry, hon. I'll have you home in twenty minutes. Unless we run into traffic."

Closing my eyes briefly, as if the gesture would numb the pain, I shook my head. "I can't wait that long. I need something now. Stop at the first store you see."

CHAPTER 7

HUDSON

The only thing my mother loved more than being right was saying *I told you so*, which made her unexpected visit a win—*for her*.

I'd spent the majority of the morning mowing the lawn, trimming shrubs, and doing every other outdoor chore I could think of to avoid being inside my own house. Don't get me wrong: I loved my mom. But right now all I wanted to do was find my softball glove and escape the Parker women as quickly as possible.

"All her life, I warned you and your father, God bless his soul, that no good would come from giving into Caryn's every whim." Mom paused from her perch on the sofa, and looked over the rim of her glasses from me to my sister. "Didn't I? Now look at her."

My gaze automatically flicked to Caryn, who was in the hot seat next to her. She appeared even more miserable than when she'd landed on my doorstep last week after a huge fight with her husband. They'd been arguing over upgrading to a bigger house in an exclusive Atlanta suburb. My natural instinct had always been to try and restore the smile to the face of the baby girl born to my parents as I was entering my teenage years.

Only Caryn wasn't that adorable baby anymore. She was twenty-three, married with a baby of her own, and although she wasn't showing yet, she had another on the way.

Sigh. And as much as it pained me to admit, Mom was absolutely right. Thanks to my late father and I, Caryn felt entitled and was accustomed to twisting the men in her life around her little finger. So when her husband refused to give in to her latest demand, she hadn't run home to our mother. Instead, her spoiled-rotten ass had packed up their daughter and made the four-hour drive from Atlanta to *my* house.

"If it weren't for you taking her in, she'd be at home working through this disagreement with her husband," Mom repeated, as if we hadn't heard her the first three times.

Probably, I thought. And for the record, I didn't like this situation, either, but what was I supposed to do? Throw Caryn and my niece out on the street?

I resumed navigating the maze of toys that had taken over my living room, paying extra attention to the area near the inflatable playpen-slash-bounce house where my two-year-old niece napped. The kid loved swiping my things, especially my phone and pricey electronic gadgets, and in the days since she and her mother had invaded my home, I'd learned to keep them out of sight and out of her reach.

Still, the precautions were no match for a determined toddler. Fiona was craftier than her mother had been at the same age, when Caryn had loved taking anything of mine that she could wrap her chubby fist around. My niece was also better at hiding her pilfered stash.

"Did either of you see Fee with my softball glove earlier?"

"Never mind your glove," my mother said, attempting to draw me into the conversation again. "We've got a family situation here, and I want to know what you're planning to do to rectify it."

Caryn sniffed. "He could build us a new house." She pinned me with her teary, doe-like eyes.

"Hudson." Mom's tone was a mix of warning and dread.

Rubbing the back of my neck, I steeled myself against the pleading in my sister's eyes. "I am not building you a house."

"You're not?" She blinked.

I shook my head slowly.

While I'd often taken Caryn's side in her battles with our mother growing up, it wasn't my place to champion her cause in disagreements with her husband. Will wasn't hitting or mistreating her. As far as I could tell, the man loved the hell out of her and his baby daughter.

"But…" Caryn whined.

I interrupted her protest. "You're welcome to stay here as long as you like, but I'm not getting in the middle of married folks business."

My mother released the breath she'd apparently been holding. "Thank goodness."

The tears welling up in Caryn's eyes rolled down her cheeks. "Don't you see? It's the perfect solution," she insisted. "If you took care of it, Will couldn't go on and on about priorities, and things that won't matter for years, like our retirement and Fiona's education. He's just being cheap and totally unreasonable."

"If you ask me, your husband is just being smart. He's looking at the bigger picture, instead of trying to impress your uppity friends and sorority sisters," Mom said.

"Nobody asked you," Caryn snapped.

"Too bad. If you had taken my advice and finished college, instead of jumping up and getting married…"

Caryn cut her off. "Don't start up with that again."

My sister had studied for two years at Tennessee State University, and then she'd surprised us all by eloping with her high-school sweetheart during the summer break before her junior year. She hadn't returned to school, and my mother was still throwing what she believed was a mistake up in my sister's face.

Here we go. I groaned inwardly. Right now, my brother-in-law would be doing me a huge favor if he came to take his wife and his mother-in-law back to Atlanta.

Where was that glove?

The two of them continued to bicker, so I stalked through the maze of baby toys littering the living room to the dining room and through to the kitchen, only to double-back to the living room again.

My gaze drifted back to my sleeping niece. I had to think like a toddler. She was a crafty one, too. Once she'd hidden my cell phone in the sofa cushions. Another time I found it on the bottom shelf of the kitchen pantry behind a box of Cheerios. It was currently in my possession, but my pricey smartwatch, tablet computer, and softball glove were all MIA.

Practice didn't start for another hour, and the park was only minutes away, but I wanted the hell out of here. I spotted the large pink diaper bag across the room where it had been dropped on the floor. Unzipping it, I smiled with relief. *Pay dirt!*

I retrieved my glove and ruffled through

the remaining contents. No watch. No tablet. Glove tucked under my arm, I made the mistake of taking another glimpse of my sister's face. Mom was on a roll with the unsolicited advice. Although it was well-intended, it had the effect of kicking someone when they were already down.

Sighing, I reached into my back pocket for my wallet and pulled out a credit card. "Take it." I held it out to Caryn. "Go buy something to cheer yourself up."

"Thank you," Caryn sniffed.

Mom harrumphed. "She doesn't need to cheer up, *she needs to grow up.*"

True. But in the meantime, a little shopping would lift my sister's spirits and soothe my guilt for abandoning her to face our mother's haranguing alone.

I walked out the back door to the garage. The sound of my pickup's engine coming to life accompanied by the radio blasting last night's sports scores were a welcome reprieve from the bickering I'd left behind.

My brain had already switched gears to softball. Even with the addition of the two college-athlete interns I'd hired yesterday and added to the team roster, we'd still need plenty of practice to win back-to-back championships.

And winning would guarantee another year of Riley Sinclair up in my face. A smile lifted the corners of my mouth as I drove to a diner between my house and the park. Mom showing up first thing this morning and immediately locking horns with Caryn had robbed me of my appetite. My growling stomach reminded me that I hadn't had more than a cup of coffee all day.

I bought a newspaper from the box outside the diner and scarfed down an afternoon meal of bacon and eggs. Walking back to my truck, I glanced at my wrist to check the time.

"Dang it, Fee," I muttered, remembering my kleptomaniac-in-training niece had swiped it.

I checked my phone instead. Practice wasn't for another half hour, which left me with some time to kill. A supermarket was located in the same shopping plaza as the diner, so I decided to grab drinks for the team. There was a cooler in the bed of my pickup that I could fill with ice to keep them cold.

I was headed to the checkout lane with my shopping cart full of bottled water and Gatorade when I remembered the ice. Making my way to the ice freezer in the back of the store, I did a double take when I saw who was standing in front of it.

Riley.

The muscles inside of my chest contracted, and I suppressed the smile threatening to break out across my lips. She retrieved a bag of ice, turned around, and frowned.

"Parker. What are you doing here?"

I'd expected the borderline-hostile greeting. It was pretty much the one I always got from her since Parker Construction had taken possession of the softball championship trophy.

Then my mouth dropped open, and I blinked. She had done something different to her hair, and she wore makeup on her usually bare face. However, it was her red swollen eyes that took me by surprise.

Instinctively, I reached out to her. My hand rested on her arm. "Are you okay? What happened?"

Her appearance roused my protective instincts. Riley was no wuss; she was one of the toughest people I'd ever met. It would take a lot to bring tears to her eyes. I wanted to rip whoever was responsible for putting them there in half.

She averted her gaze. "I'm fine."

But she obviously wasn't, and I intended to get to the bottom of it. "Did someone hurt you?" I asked through clenched teeth. I was struggling to keep a lid on the rage bubbling up inside me until I knew who to direct it at.

Touching my fingertip to her chin, I lifted it until she met my gaze. "Tell me, Riley. Who made you cry?"

She blinked. Her big brown eyes registered surprise, and then softened. For a brief moment, it appeared as if she was touched by my concern.

Then she suddenly knocked away my

finger. "*I* don't cry, Parker," she said. "I make grown men cry. Just like you're going to do when I come to retrieve that championship softball trophy from your offices."

Relief flooded me. *This* was more like the Riley I knew and couldn't help but like. Still, something was going on with her.

I studied her face. Upon closer examination, I realized that although the skin around her eyebrows was red and swollen, her actual eyes were clear, albeit a touch watery. My gaze drifted to the items clutched in her arms: extra-strength aspirin, aloe vera gel, and the bag of ice.

"Did you injure yourself?"

"Hell, no," she barked out, and then winced.

I curbed the instinct to touch her again. Her vehement protest belied the way she gingerly held her body. She shifted uncomfortably, as if she ached all over.

"Are you sure you aren't hurt?" I asked.

"You'd like that, wouldn't you, Parker?" she asked. "With me sidelined, there'd be nothing stopping you from winning and holding onto that softball trophy for another year."

Raising my hands, I took a step backward. "Hey, something is obviously wrong. I was just concerned."

She advanced on me and pointed a finger at my chest. For the first time, I noticed her usually plain nails were painted a glossy red.

"You can't fool me with that phony concern. It won't get in my head and throw me off my game. Nor will flashing those sexy bedroom eyes of yours in my face get me in your kitchen naked, asking how you like your eggs."

Spinning on her heels, Riley limped away, leaving me momentarily stunned. *Well, I'll be damned.* She *had* overheard what I'd said the other night. She also thought my eyes were sexy. This time I couldn't suppress the smile that touched my lips. Riley Sinclair wasn't as unaffected by me as she pretended to be.

CHAPTER 8

RILEY

Rolling my eyes, I exhaled an exasperated sigh. "It's been over a week now. How long are you going to gawk at me like I'm a stranger?"

Cal shook his head. "You sound like Riley, and you work just as hard as she does, but you certainly don't look like her lately."

The reaction to my spruced-up appearance had been the exact same every day, at every one of our construction sites. The grooves on my face deepened along with my frown. If I wasn't careful, the Delilah app was soon going to suggest a shot of Botox.

"My eyes are up here, Cal," I pointed out. Thankfully, his gaze traveled up from my Big Guns–assisted boobs to my face.

"Um...sorry," he muttered sheepishly. "I'm still not used to you in pink. Yeah, it's the pink."

The night of my makeover, I'd sat on a bag

of ice at the computer while Plum and I clicked our way through the online boutique for tradeswomen. An overnight shipment later, and I had a new work wardrobe that was both pink and functional. More importantly, the clothes fit. No more having to make do with shapeless jeans and shirts.

I interrupted Cal's stammering explanation. "The first inspection of the building is tomorrow, and I need to check the plumbers' work."

Back to business, my project manager gave me a progress report on the Espresso building as I looked over the work Owen's crews from Mill's Plumbing had done so far. As we walked through the site, I couldn't help wish my dad were here to see all the upgrades and improvements.

"Good work, Cal." I went on to explain that I'd be tied up at another site tomorrow, and it was doubtful I'd be here for the inspection.

He nodded as we made our way back to the ground floor of the building. "You coming to the game this evening?" he asked.

I was about to shake my head, but then I remembered Parker Construction was up tonight. They were playing Stellar Electric. So far, they'd only lost one game this season, the same as us. "I'll try to stop by. You?"

Cal nodded. "Figured I'd bring the boys along and give the wife a break," he said. "Should be a competitive game. Stellar has a pretty good team this year."

"Of ringers," I snorted. "I doubt half of the so-called employees on their team know how to plug a lamp in a socket, never mind rewire one."

Damned ringers irked the hell out of me, especially because as head of the company, my mother would never allow an employee on the payroll that didn't pull their weight. The softball field didn't count.

"It'll be interesting to see if Parker's team can pull it out. I know he's hoping for back-to-back championships."

"Humph." I thought about bumping into Parker at the store the weekend before last, and how I noticed those seductive bedroom eyes of his for the first time. Fortunately, it had been a case of temporary insanity on my part, and I had quickly came to my senses. "He can forget about that."

On the ground floor, my gaze automatically drifted across the street. I didn't need to check my watch to know it was nearly time: the man I'd put myself through the hellish *Operation Delilah* for was about to make his after-work appearance.

Today's the day, Riley. I gave myself a mental pep talk as I walked over to the chain-link fence to stand sentinel. You will not punk out this time. *You're going to march across the street and do exactly what this app you're paying five bucks a month for advises.*

In the component of the app dedicated to approaching a man, the television heroine had a list of what she'd dubbed "proven tactics." I decided to try asking him for the time or for directions. Once he answered my question, Delilah advised keeping the conversation going no matter what. Then I was supposed to give him my phone number, or even better, ask him out on the spot.

"Uh, Riley?"

Dragging my attention away from the building across the street, I turned to see Deke standing next to me. His hands were shoved into the front pockets of his jeans, and he wore a shy, very un-Deke-like expression on his face.

"What's up?" I asked. Despite the things I'd overheard him say about me at First Down a few weeks ago after one beer too many, my first reaction was concern.

"Everything okay with you?" I asked when he didn't respond to my first question.

"Yeah, I'm cool." He looked down at his work boots before facing me again.

"For goodness sake, spit it out, Deke. What do you want, an advance on your salary? A day off?" He was a hard worker, so it wouldn't be a problem to accommodate him.

He shook his head. "Nothing like that. I...well...it's just that you look so different. It's like I'm seeing you for the first time, and I was wondering if you'd like to go out to dinner?"

"Together?" Call me slow, but I didn't quite grasp his meaning.

He nodded. "Of course. How about this weekend? You free Saturday night?"

What? Your dick got a death wish?

I thought about his reference to me, but kept my mouth shut. Unlike Parker, Deke would never know I'd overheard him. Besides, that kind of talk had no place on a Sinclair work site. Neither did a romantic relationship with someone who worked for me.

"I don't date men I work with," I said simply. Not that any had ever asked me out before now. My attention was again drawn to the other side of the street, where I hoped to soon see the man I *did* want to date.

Deke shrugged. "Okay, but if you change your mind, my offer stands."

I didn't even notice him leave. The pounding noise of jackhammers busting through concrete at a neighboring work site was also lost on me. I stood at the fence barricading the Espresso building, waiting. I recalled the segment of the app I'd played on repeat the last few nights and silently rehearsed my approach.

Excuse me, sir. Would you happen to have the time? Uh, and maybe you'd also like to have dinner with me?

"Gawd, he's going to think I'm the biggest weirdo ever," I grumbled aloud.

Retrieving my phone from the back pocket of my jeans, I consulted the app one last time. Delilah filled the small screen. "Any action is better than no action," she advised. "Just walk up to him and introduce yourself. If you've taken my advice on ramping up your look, don't worry, gorgeous. *He'll do all the talking.*"

I checked my face in the mirror app Delilah had suggested adding to my phone. There were no signs of dirt or concrete dust, and the makeup I'd touched up in my truck on the way to the Espresso building site had fared well.

I jammed the phone back into my pocket. My breath caught in my chest when the double doors of his office building swung open. My dream man strode out, and the staccato beat of my pulse drowned out everything else. He wore his typical work uniform of a suit. This one was tan with a pale-green shirt and tie. He was talking on the phone, his ever-present earbuds jammed in his ears.

"You can do this. You can do this," I whispered. My gaze was glued to his every movement until something, or more specifically, *someone*, caught my eye.

A guy wearing an orange baseball cap and huge sunglasses covering half his face was shadowing my mystery crush. Uneasiness crept over me as the baseball-cap-clad man looked suspiciously from side to side. Out of nowhere, he delivered a sucker punch to the back of Mr. Perfect's head. The man I hadn't had the nerve to introduce myself to crumpled to the ground under the weight of the unexpected blow.

"Oh, shit!" I ran toward them, only to be thwarted by cars speeding down the street, separating me from the crime unfolding right before my eyes. Racket from the surrounding construction sites muted my furious shouts. The mugger, who had already taken the fallen man's leather messenger bag, started to rifle through his suit jacket pockets.

I made my way across the street, dodging the bumpers of the moving cars. The blaring horns and epithets from drivers scrambling to their suburban homes were lost on me. My pink hard hat was also lost in the mad dash. By the time I got to the other side, the mugger had punched Mr. Perfect again. Then he yanked the wallet from his back pocket and ran.

I crouched beside my crush, the man I'd been watching for weeks. He looked dazed, but fortunately he was still conscious. "You okay?"

"My laptop. My phone. All of my business..." He attempted to get up from the ground, and then immediately grabbed his head and winced in pain. "A-all of my work," he stammered.

"I'll try to get them back." I stood, and then shouted at the few people who had finally noticed something was wrong. "Somebody call for help!"

The guy in the orange cap hadn't gotten far. I spotted him a few blocks ahead. He was no longer running, just walking briskly; apparently he was confident his victim was too dazed to pursue him.

I took off after him. Adrenaline and outrage at the crime I'd witnessed fueled me as I pushed and shoved my way through the mass exodus of workers abandoning the surrounding office and government buildings.

My eyes trained on the orange cap, it didn't take long for me to close the gap between us. I reached out, only a split second from grabbing the mugger. He looked over his shoulder, and spotting me, he broke into a run.

"Stop!" I shouted breathlessly, still giving chase.

I somehow managed to get within a few feet of him again, but not quite close enough. I was determined not to let him get away, though. Diving forward, I crashed into him with all my might. Momentum sent us both hurtling toward the pavement, with the mugger taking the brunt of the impact. He hit the ground first, and I landed on top of him.

"Crazy, bitch!" He shoved me off of him.

"I'll show you crazy!" Anger surged through me. It had less to do with my mystery crush and more to do with not letting this cowardly bastard get away with attacking someone in broad daylight. He had taken something that didn't belong to him. "You lowdown, thieving..."

We struggled on the sidewalk, and I clung to the stolen messenger bag slung across his body to keep him from escaping. He raised his fist to take a swing at me, but unlike the unsuspecting man he'd hit from behind, I saw it coming and jerked my head out of the way.

The fist intended for my face smashed into the concrete instead, and the mugger's howl of pain filled the air. Still clutching the messenger bag strap with one hand, I grabbed his shirt with my other hand and pulled myself to my knees.

"Somebody call the police!" I yelled between sucking in gasps of air. Sweat ran down my face. Regular runs and my job kept me pretty fit, but they hadn't prepared me for brawling in the street, and I doubted I could keep my precarious hold on this guy much longer.

Finally I saw a beat cop running toward us on foot, along with Cal and Deke, while sirens wailed in the background. Relief whooshed through me. The mugger must have seen them, too. He managed to yank his shirt free of my grasp, so I grabbed the messenger bag with both hands to hold on to him.

"Let me go, dammit!" he demanded.

I tightened my grip. "You're not going anywhere!"

A rusty Pontiac screeched to a stop at the corner. "Hurry up, man!" the driver shouted. "Cops are coming!"

Once again, the mugger tried to pull away from me, but I stubbornly refused to let go. The driver revved the engine in warning.

"Screw it." The mugger pulled the strap over his head and shoved the leather bag at me. It hit me so hard that I fell backward on my panty-less ass.

He dived into the passenger seat of the Pontiac, and the rusted-out car burned rubber speeding up a side street. Seconds later, Cal, Deke, and the cops surrounded me. All of them were too late to be of any real help.

"You all right?" Cal stuck out his hand.

I grabbed ahold of it, pulled myself up, and then wiped my palms against my now-torn jeans. "Yeah, but he got away."

"What in the world possessed you to go after a mugger in the first place?" Cal scolded. "Apparently he knocked the hell out the guy he robbed. He could have done the same to you."

Deke nodded. "Situation could have gone south real quick."

The beat cop echoed the same admonishing words as my crew. Assured that I was indeed okay, Cal and Deke returned to the Espresso building site while I gave the cops as much information as I could.

"Do you think you'll be able to track them down?" I asked.

The cop nodded. "Your descriptions of the suspects, combined with providing us with the make and license plate number on the car, is the biggest break we've had in weeks."

The spot where the attack had taken place was now swarming with flashing blue lights. An ambulance was also on the scene. "The man who was robbed, he all right?" I asked one of the other cops.

An officer sporting a shaved head and a protruding stomach that strained the buttons on his uniform replied. "The paramedics are treating him now, but it looks like just a few scrapes and a bump on the head."

I handed him the messenger bag. "Could you make sure he gets this back?"

After chasing the mugger and rolling around on the sidewalk, my jeans and pink T-shirt were a disaster. My hair and makeup probably hadn't fared much better. I didn't need to consult an app on my phone to know I'd shot to hell any chance of making a good impression on anyone today.

Thanks to my impulsiveness and stupidity, the mission Plum had dubbed Operation Delilah had all been for nothing. I stared at the ground as I trudged back to the

Espresso building site. I couldn't even hold on to the bad guy.

"Hold up, Ms. Sinclair."

I turned, expecting to see the cop who had interviewed me earlier. Maybe he had a question he'd forgotten to ask. Instead, the man I'd been hung up on for weeks jogged toward me. My heartbeat, which had finally slowed to its normal pace after going all badass on that mugger, slammed against my chest so hard I thought my ribs would crack.

He'd shed his suit jacket, and his shirtsleeves were rolled up. The bandage on his forehead and the smudge of dirt across his cheek didn't distract from his looks. Up close, he was even more handsome. *Damn, this guy really was Mr. Perfect.*

He rested a hand on my bare arm. "The cops gave me your name. I wanted to thank you for getting my bag back. Fortunately, the guy who took it had stuck my phone inside," he said. "You shouldn't have gone after him, but I really can't thank you enough for what you did."

I stood there ogling him like a damn fool. After weeks of longing for this moment, I couldn't believe he was actually talking to me. His gorgeous lips were moving, but I swear I didn't hear a word coming out of them.

"Ms. Sinclair, are you all right?" he asked. "Do you need the paramedics to take a look at you?"

He squeezed my forearm, and I blinked.

I finally found my voice. "Uh…I'm good, thanks. And my name is Riley."

He smiled, displaying teeth so perfect they must have made some dentist a fortune. "Nice to meet you, Riley. I'm Ian King."

The name fit the man. I licked my suddenly dry lips.

"A thank-you seems inadequate after the way you came to my rescue back there," he continued. "I was hoping to repay you with dinner, or maybe we could go for coffee?"

For weeks I'd rehearsed asking him out, and here he was asking me. But his invitation didn't bring me the elation I should have felt. It was only out of a sense of obligation, and as much as I wanted him, I wasn't that hard up.

"That's not necessary, Mr. King. I was glad to help."

"Oh, it's *very necessary.*" He insisted I call him Ian as his gaze slid down to check out my barren ring finger. I went tingly all over. "I'm intrigued by a woman who goes to the lengths you did to help a stranger, and I'd love to get to know you better, Riley Sinclair. Have dinner with me tomorrow night?"

He wanted to get to know me? I swallowed hard and opened my mouth to accept his offer, but then remembered I had a game. We played Green Tree Landscapers tomorrow night. "Sorry, I can't tomorrow."

"How about Thursday?" he asked.

I nodded. My insides felt as fizzy as a freshly uncorked bottle of champagne.

"Then it's a date," he said. "Looking forward to it already, Riley."

I was, too. I couldn't wait to tell Plum. It looked like I had somewhere to wear my get 'em girl dress after all.

CHAPTER 9

HUDSON

After spending the day traveling between several Parker Construction projects around town, I went into the office to start on paperwork that honestly could have waited. Alicia and the rest of the office staff had cleared out hours ago, so it was quiet, and I could think.

Unlike my home nowadays, where Caryn was still camped out pouting.

Over the weekend, I'd finally caved in and reached out to my brother-in-law. Not to ask him to buy Caryn a bigger house as she'd requested, but to find out when the hell he was going to put an end to this standoff and come for his family.

I got nowhere. Will told me that after giving in to my sister on every point since they'd married, he couldn't acquiesce on this one. With a new baby on the way, Caryn was going to have to learn how to live within their means.

As much as I adored my baby sister, I understood where the guy was coming from. Still, I wish the two of them would handle their marital issues in-house, more specifically, *in their house*.

I looked up from contracts the company's attorney had sent over by messenger for my signature. The gleaming trophies on the credenza caught my eye. As always, they roused thoughts of Riley. Standing, I walked to the window behind my ancient desk and peered through the blinds. It was nearly six, but the summer sun shone through the tops of the trees strategically scattered throughout the office park.

Nearly two weeks had passed since my strange encounter with her at the store. I'd hoped to see her again the other night at our game. Cal Webber and a few guys from Sinclair Construction's team had come out to witness us trounce Stellar Electric, but not Riley.

The new interns had done well. The one from Vanderbilt had hit a home run, while the Tennessee State University biology major had made a double play in the bottom of the sixth inning that resulted in two outs.

Riley's absence had put a damper on an otherwise-sweet victory. It also temporarily shelved my plan to finally make a move on her.

A client had given me tickets to see a

comedian that was doing a show at the Tennessee Performing Arts Center, and I wanted to ask her to go with me. Staring through the window at the treetops, I exhaled. Who knew when I'd run into Riley again? Even when I did, people always surrounded us, and I probably wouldn't be able to talk to her privately.

Screw it. I didn't care who was around. The next time I saw Riley Sinclair, I planned to tell her exactly where I stood. Let the chips fall where they may.

"Parker!"

I froze. The sound of my name being yelled in that familiar voice made me question my sanity. Geez, I had it bad. Now my mind was playing tricks on me.

"Did you think I wouldn't find out?"

The angry question shattered the peaceful atmosphere of my office, and a smile tugged at the corners of my mouth. This was no daydream. The Riley of my fantasies was soft and yielding, with a hidden vulnerability she only revealed to me, while the real Riley was...

"I know you hear me, Parker."

I turned toward the voice and did a double take. Riley's sudden appearance in my office wasn't the only surprise.

Dayum!

I pressed my lips together to keep the expletive from escaping. I'd expected to see a pissed-off Riley, and sure enough she sported the scowl my face seemed to trigger.

"Riley?" For the second time in minutes, I didn't trust my senses. A glimpse of the woman standing in my office doorway was usually enough to turn me on, but looking at her now had me hot enough to catch fire.

She wore a dress the color of cotton candy. The thin fabric looked as if it would disintegrate at the slightest touch. I wanted to touch it, bad. My gaze drifted to her breasts, positioned a few inches below her chin, and lingered. I wanted to touch them, too.

"Hey, Parker!" Riley snapped her fingers. "My eyes are up here."

I reluctantly lifted my gaze and noticed she'd changed her hairstyle, too. Her dreadlocks were secured on top of her head in a straitlaced bun. The prim hairdo was a stark contrast to the sexy dress and strappy, high-heeled shoes, and I battled an overwhelming urge to free the ropes of her hair and fist them in my hand.

And those shoes. The only thing I liked better than looking at her in them was imagining the heels digging into my back as she draped her legs over my shoulders or wrapped those thick thighs tight around my waist.

"I'm on to you," Riley snapped.

Letting out an unsteady breath, I walked to the front of my desk and leaned against it. "Good to see you, too, but you didn't have to get all dressed up to pay me a visit. Casual would have been fine."

I crossed my arms over my chest. My outward cool belied my utter delight at seeing her.

"Don't be ridiculous," she snorted as she stalked toward me. "I have a date tonight."

A date. The words hit me like a punch in the gut. I thought back to the guys talking about her in the sports bar. They'd all relegated Riley to the "friend only" category.

Apparently, someone else had other ideas, and he'd been smart enough to beat me to it and ask her out.

"Who?" I blurted out, any pretense of playing it cool forgotten.

Riley didn't hear me. Her gaze had drifted over to the credenza and the trophies she wanted so badly. Right now, I didn't give a damn about them. All I could think about was that it might be too late for me. That is, if I'd even had a chance with her in the first place.

"Did you think I wouldn't find out about those so-called new interns of yours?" She didn't wait for an answer, but inched closer until she was all up in my face. "I heard all about how those ringers insured your victory over Stellar Electric the other night. So I made it my business to stop by here to let you know I was on to your lowdown, slick..."

She continued bitching, but it was lost on me. All I could focus on were those full, lightly glossed lips. The berry tint was reminiscent of summer fruit, and I wondered if they tasted as good as they looked.

"Shut up, Riley!"

She froze mid-rant. "What did you just say to me?" Her eyes widened and then narrowed. "Cause I couldn't have heard you right."

Wrapping an arm around her waist, I hauled her against me. I felt the whoosh of her next breath leave her body as our gazes locked. "I said *shut up*."

She stared up at me, unblinking. Her palms were splayed against my chest, but she hadn't pushed me away, *yet*. "Just what in the hell do you think you're doing, Parker?" She tried to sound outraged, but her voice lacked the bluster she'd used since she'd landed at my door.

"What I want to do every time I see you."

Her pretty lips, only a fraction of an inch from mine, parted in surprise, and I took full advantage. Leaning in, I captured that brash mouth of hers in a kiss. No soft or tentative peck. I went all in. I wanted to leave no doubt in her mind as to the all-consuming desire she evoked in me.

Riley stiffened, and then squirmed in my arms, and I mentally prepared myself to be shoved away, or knowing her, knocked the hell out at any moment. Instead, she responded with a low moan in her throat. The muffled sound of sweet surrender went straight to my groin as her body melted into mine.

Her hands moved to my shoulders, and she clutched them with her fingertips, as if she needed to hang on to stay upright. She had no worries in that department. Holding her flush against me, I savored the long-awaited taste of her mouth. My tongue stroked hers as my hardness nudged her belly, making it clear her mouth wasn't the only thing I wanted to explore this evening.

And I wasn't the only one.

Her nipples pebbled beneath the thin fabric of her dress as she ground against me. Her arms encircled my neck and she deepened the kiss, sucking my tongue in a way that made my toes curl inside my Timberland's. My dick instantly turned to concrete.

Her fervor was the unspoken permission I needed.

There had always been tension in the air when Riley and I were in the same room, but this was different. It wasn't driven by hostility or competition, but an overpowering longing that made me forget everything except the two of us right here. *Right now.*

I grabbed her ass with both hands and squeezed it through the thin fabric of her dress. She moaned again and rocked her hips against mine. Just when I thought I couldn't get any harder, I did.

In one swift motion, I lifted the woman

I've wanted for so long off her feet. I sat her on top of the metal desk and positioned myself between her legs without breaking the kiss that had definitely been worth the wait.

My hand moved to her dreads, instantly finding the pins anchoring the bun she'd tamed them into. I freed the ropes of hair and luxuriated in the velvet feel of them against my fingers.

Finally, as the kiss ended, our gazes collided. The brown eyes that had always stared daggers at me were now dazed by lust. Her guard had dropped, and I could see past the hard chocolate shell guarding her emotions to the soft gooey center.

I could have stared into her eyes for hours, but the notion was overruled by my need to touch and taste every inch of her. Fisting the locked strands of her hair in my hands, I tugged her head back and licked the throbbing pulse point on her throat.

"Yes," Riley rasped in a voice I barely recognized.

My face was buried in her neck, but I was already hotly anticipating tossing those long legs over my shoulders and burying my tongue between her thighs.

Riley palmed my erection, and just like that, my plan changed. I kissed her neck once more and pulled back. I glanced down at her hand stroking me through my pants and then up to her glazed-over eyes.

"I'm going to fuck you until the only date you'll want to go on tonight is to my bedroom."

A wicked gleam sparkled in her eyes. She opened her mouth, and I waited for her sassy response. A beat passed, and she blinked. It was as if someone had snapped their fingers and awakened her from a hypnotic trance. "Oh, no. My date! I have a date tonight!"

The hand massaging my dick abruptly stopped.

No. No. No. No. No. I mentally kicked myself for triggering her memory with the word *date*.

I could see the wheels in her head spinning as she tried to reconcile the fact that when she walked through my office door, all she'd wanted to hold were the coveted trophies sitting on the credenza. Now she was holding *me*. A whole lot of me.

She snatched her hand away from my crotch. Still perched on my desk, she ran her fingers through her wild tangle of locs. "I-I can't. I mean, we can't."

"Yeah, we can," I said on behalf of my hard-on. "Admit it, Riley. You want me."

She glared back at me. "Don't flatter yourself."

I cocked a brow. "What man wouldn't be flattered to have you on the verge of shoving your hands down his jeans?"

She snorted, but her telltale face turned an interesting shade of red. "Y-you can just kiss my…" She held up her hands and shook her head. "Nope. I'm not even going there with you right now, Parker. I have a date tonight and nothing is going to ruin it."

Hopping off my desk, she squeezed past me in an angry huff. The next thing I heard was the sound of fabric ripping. I'm not sure what surprised me more—half a pink dress hanging from the jagged edge of my desk, or *my spectacular view of Riley Sinclair's bare ass.*

CHAPTER 10

RILEY

"Damn!"

Parker and I muttered the expletive at the same time. Only he wasn't the one naked from the waist down.

I scrambled behind one of the chairs facing his desk for cover. Its high back shielded my exposed goods from his thirsty eyes. Unfortunately, it didn't keep me from ogling the bulge in his jeans. I pressed my lips together to keep from licking them. I pressed my legs together at the memory of caressing his rock-hard heat through the well-worn denim.

He'd been right. I had been on the verge of shoving my hand down his pants, and that was just for starters. *What the hell was the matter with me?*

"Hey, Riley!" Parker snapped his fingers, and I blinked. "My eyes are up here."

Just when I thought nothing could be more embarrassing than having my ass out in my rival's office, he'd caught me leering at his junk. I delivered my most menacing scowl, the one I used to show the mostly-male crews working for Sinclair that I meant business.

Parker met it with a raised brow. The mouth that had kissed me until I was weak in the knees twisted into an amused smirk. "No panties and a Brazilian, huh?" His smirk stretched into a dimple-revealing smile as he stroked the day's worth of beard clinging to his chin. *"Sweet."*

"Could you please just hand me the other half of my dress?" I needed to cover my behind and get the hell out of here.

The spark in his eyes dimmed. "Yeah, sure." He reached over and tugged at the flimsy material.

"And be careful!"

Too late.

I tried to block out the sound of fabric tearing, but it echoed in my ears as I watched the remainder of my dress fall to the carpet in shreds. Double damn. I ran a frustrated hand through my locs.

"Sorry about that," he said. But he didn't appear apologetic as he resumed leaning against that damned dress-shredding desk. I rolled my eyes at his casual stance.

"Do you have a jacket or something I could put on to walk out of here, so I can drive home and change?"

He shrugged. "All I have is the shirt on my back."

"Well, give it to me." I held my hand out, expecting him to take off the polo shirt and toss it my direction. His height, along with the span of those wide shoulders, would easily make what served as a shirt for him a short dress for me. There would be enough material to cover both my Brazilian and backside.

Ignoring my outstretched hand, he pushed off the desk and ambled toward me. I held my breath as he stood in front of my chair and slowly undid the shirt's three buttons. Then he pulled it up and over his head.

Lawd have mercy. I gawked at his well-muscled torso. Goosebumps of excitement erupted on my skin, and I fought the urge to explore the ridges of that taunt six-pack with my fingertips, closely followed by my tongue.

He's not your type. He's not your type.

I silently repeated my mantra, but the taste of him lingered on my lips. Despite my silent protest, I wanted more. More of his kisses. More of his strong embrace. More of what I'd had my hands on just moments ago. I dug my nails into my palms to keep from reaching for him again.

Efforts to conjure up images of Mr. Perfect, who I was supposed to have dinner with later this evening, fell flat. At the moment, what my heart wanted took a backseat to what my body craved.

Parker held the shirt out, just slightly out of my reach. "It's yours if you want it." His deep voice rumbled through me, and I could feel the heat radiating off his naked chest. "Unless there's something I have that you want even more..."

He trained those dark eyes on me, and I diverted my gaze before I got caught up in them—and him—more than I already was. I'd made it clear to everyone that he wasn't my type. I didn't even like him...did I?

The rational side of my brain finally broke through the effect of his bedroom eyes and the who-the-hell-knew-he-could-kiss-like-that mojo Parker was slinging my way.

Get moving, girl, my common sense shouted. *Take that shirt dangling off his finger, put it on, and get the hell out of here. And whatever you do, do not glance down at option two.*

But I couldn't help it. Not taking another long look at my long and hard second choice would have been akin to not licking an ice cream cone on a sweltering summer day. Whoa. Bad analogy. *Very bad.*

Frowning, I looked pointedly at the shirt and then met his gaze head-on. "You know which one I want, Parker."

"Then take it."

Any attempts at modesty forgotten, I abandoned the cover provided by the office chair. His eyes widened as he stared at my

Brazilian in a way that nearly made it worth the torture. I grasped his waistband and pulled him closer, then undid the top button of his jeans. My Delilah Cole badass-ness put a smile on his kissable mouth. I returned it with one of my own.

He flung the proffered shirt across the room. "Good choice."

I looked from the zipper I was dragging down over the huge bulge in his jeans. "It had *better* be good."

My rival cocked a brow at the challenge. He stilled my eager hands, and then went to his office door and pushed it closed. The lock clicked into place, sending a shiver of anticipation shimmying down my back.

He loosened his bootlaces before toeing off his work boots and shedding his socks. My teeth sank into my bottom lip when his jeans and underwear hit the floor in one swoop. If I'd worn panties, they surely would have melted right off at the sight of him walking toward me in all his fully aroused glory.

"Like what you see?"

Oh, I liked it. No matter how much I tried not to. The warmth from his big body surrounded me moments before he took me into his arms. I rested a hand on the dark skin of his chest and looked into his eyes. There was something we needed to be clear on before we took things any further. "This changes nothing between us, Parker. I still can't stand you."

Undeterred, he rocked his hips against mine, and I groaned as his erection pressed against my belly. "When we're done, you won't be able to stand. Period."

"I'm serious." I tried again. "This is a one-time..."

"Riley," he cut me off.

My gaze focused on his lips. "What?"

"Shut up." Leaning down, he covered my mouth with his, shutting down the conversation and any thoughts I had outside his embrace.

The kiss was long and slow. Each stroke of his tongue drew me in deeper, and suddenly I couldn't recall why this man irked me so much, or the reason I'd even came to his office in the first place. I sighed into Parker's mouth as his tongue continued to work its magic. Why did he have to taste so damn good?

When the kiss ended, my back hugged the wall and my hands were all over his naked ass. The very butt Plum and Hope had drooled over. If they'd thought it looked good in a pair of low-slung jeans, they should experience it without them.

Parker lowered his gaze. "I want to see all of you," he said. "Take off the rest of that dress, before I tear it off."

Reluctantly, I released my grip on his firm behind. He stepped back, and although he was mere inches away, I missed the feel of his body against mine. I shed what was left of my get 'em girl dress, followed by my Big Guns bra.

I thought he might be disappointed at the sight of my breasts without the boost of padding and underwire, but I was wrong. An approving glint sparked in his seductive brown eyes, which were illuminated by the early evening sun peeking through the window blinds.

"Damn." His hushed tone was filled with awe. "You're every bit as beautiful as I imagined."

The smart-aleck comeback I always had at the ready where this man was concerned evaded me. He brushed his lips against mine. The butterfly kiss belied the urgency of his big dick pressed against my belly. Clasping my wrists in one large hand, he raised them above my head and pinned them to the wall behind me. The move offered up my breasts, which ached for his attention.

Parker's free hand slid down my body, lingering on my breasts before slowly gliding down to my rib cage and then my waist. He had the touch of a man who worked hard for his money, and I felt every rough callus on the palm caressing my hip.

Leaning in, he flicked his tongue over a beaded nipple as he parted my thighs and slipped a finger inside me. I sucked in a breath, and my head lolled. The explosion of sensations generated by both his tongue and his fingers made my entire body tingle with pleasure.

"You're so tight. So wet." His shadow of beard scraped my cheek as he kissed and nuzzled the spot between my neck and collarbone. I rocked with the rhythm of his finger. "You do want me, don't you, Riley?"

"Don't flatter yourself, Parker." The words, spoken between my breathless pants, didn't pack much punch.

He took my nipple between his teeth and gently tugged. "Am I?" His thumb slid over my clit as his finger went deeper.

I bit back a groan, leaving his question hanging in the air. My body's reaction to his touch was my answer.

Apparently, it wasn't enough.

"I want to hear it from your lips." He continued to fuck me with his finger. "Tell me you want me."

He knew damn well I did. My slippery wetness told him with every stroke of his finger.

"Just three easy words." His voice dropped an octave. "I want you."

My hands still confined over my head, I pressed my lips closed and shook my head. Unfortunately, I couldn't stifle the low moan in my throat as I writhed against the steady rhythm of his hand.

"If it's so impossible for you to say, then I have to assume you aren't interested." His finger brushed across my swollen clit as he started to withdraw it.

"Don't." The plea pushed its way out of my mouth.

His finger slid back inside me, this time deeper. "Don't what?"

"Don't stop." Lust overruled my innate impulse to oppose this man on any and everything. *"Please."*

Parker's eyes locked on mine, and he slowly shook his head. "While *please* is usually the magic word, it won't work this time." The rumble of his voice made my bare skin tingle as he once again withdrew his finger and ground his hips against mine, his erection eager to finish the job his hand had started. "So stop being a stubborn ass and just say it."

His dick twitched against my belly, and my resolve, much like the dress on the floor, shredded to pieces.

"I want you." The whispered words echoed between us as if I'd shouted them.

He kissed me long and slow. Somehow I managed not to slide down the wall when he released me only long enough to retrieve a condom from his wallet. He cradled my ass in his large hands, and my legs automatically encircled his waist. He nudged my opening, and I closed my eyes in anticipation of the ride.

"Riley."

I opened my eyes. "You've already made me practically beg. What else could we possibly have to say?"

"Just remember, I like my eggs sunny-side up and my bacon crisp."

I snorted. "Don't be ridiculous."

He plunged inside me with one sure stroke, and the sound of my screaming his name reverberated off the office walls. In that instant, the idea of standing naked in his kitchen over a frying pan didn't seem so crazy after all.

CHAPTER 11

HUDSON

Despite what had gone down in my office, I didn't feel like the guy who had gotten the girl.

I was driving home, and I guessed Riley was at her place getting ready for her date, *again*. If she looked half as good as she had when she'd stormed into my office, any guy with a pair would want to do exactly what I'd done with her.

And there wasn't a damn thing I could do about it.

All I could do was hope. Hope that I'd put it on her so good, all she'd be able to think about while sitting in some overrated restaurant with another man was *me*. I wanted her to remember how I made her knees buckle with just one kiss. I wanted her to think about how she'd dug her nails into my shoulders when I'd hit it up against the wall.

Images of us together overwhelmed me as I exited the interstate and drove along the side streets to my house. Riley's scent still clung to my body, and the sweet taste of her kisses lingered on my tongue. I also hoped that despite what she'd said about it being a one-time thing, she would also want more. Alicia had been wrong this time. Screwing Riley Sinclair's brains out definitely hadn't gotten her out of my system.

I made a right turn.

"What the...?"

Cars lined the street in front of my house. They also occupied my driveway. The sun had set and daylight was dwindling, but I could see balloons tied to my mailbox. One of them was emblazoned with the words *Party Tonight!*

I circled the block in search of a parking space. By the time I'd slid my truck into a free spot around the corner, I was pissed. It had been a long day. All I wanted to do was shower, eat dinner, and catch the Braves game on television.

Family or not, this uninvited houseguest bullshit was getting old, I thought as I stalked down the street. Still, I wouldn't kick my sister and Fee out, even if my mom did think it was the best thing I could do for them.

The sound of loud talking and raucous laughter greeted me at the edge of my yard. I trudged to my open front door and walked inside. A hoard of women had taken over my living room and apparently my dining room and kitchen, too. The champagne was flowing, and Caryn and her friends were giggling, exploring an inventory of large cardboard boxes spilling over with lingerie and sex toys.

Great. I exhaled, trying to tap in to my nearly depleted patience. There was a dildo party going on at my place, and since I'd been dumb enough to give Caryn my credit card earlier, odds were I was paying for it, too.

CHAPTER 12

RILEY

Plum grabbed the remote and muted the television as soon as the first commercial aired. She sat back on the sofa next to Hope, and they both stared at me with expectant faces.

Squirming in the armchair adjacent to them, I took a big gulp from my wineglass. The fruity Moscato was the same understated shade of pale pink as the interior of Hope's condo. We were supposed to be watching the season finale of *Hot Mess*, but my best friend and sister were more interested in my business than Delilah Cole's latest affair.

I was still reeling from the events of last night. I'd had dinner with the man I'd spent weeks worshipping from afar, and I'd also had Hudson Parker. In fact, I'd had so much of Parker, that when we were done, I'd staggered out of his office like a zombie. A dick-dizzy zombie clad only in heels and his oversized shirt.

"Don't keep us in suspense. How was the big date with Mr. Perfect?" Plum asked.

Hope sniffed. "I can't believe no one even bothered to tell me Mr. Perfect existed or fill me in on this app business until tonight," she said. "I could have helped with your big makeover."

I put my wineglass on the coffee table and selected a cucumber sandwich from the tiered silver tray, ignoring the floral-trimmed china plate my sister had placed in front of me. Hope would have choked on her pearls at the app's advice to go commando. My lack of panties had definitely been a contributing factor when I ended up pinned to my rival's office wall, begging for all he had to give and more.

"Well?" Hope asked.

"Actually, his name is Ian. Ian King," I said, resetting my mental circuit breaker from Parker to the man Plum had dubbed *Mr. Perfect*. I took in my sister's hurt face. Sure, we were total opposites, but we were also tight, and I hadn't intentionally left her out of the loop. "Don't go getting your granny panties in a knot. I would have told you, but every time I came by the office, you were either away from your desk or tied up in meetings."

Hope sighed. "With Mom away on that world cruise, the office has been so crazy," she admitted.

I inclined my head toward the television mounted over the fireplace. Delilah was strutting across the flat screen in the same heels I'd worn to Parker's office. I gulped. "Um…the show is back on."

Plum aimed the remote at the TV, but instead of taking it off mute, she set the DVR to record. Then she selected two petit fours from the tray and plopped them onto a china plate. "*Hot Mess* can wait. I want to hear all about *your* hot date." She popped one of the tiny cakes in her mouth, staring at me while she chewed.

Hope nodded. "Quit stalling and start talking, Riley," she said. "We want to hear all about this Ian King."

"We went to dinner at that new Asian fusion restaurant south of town."

"Really!" Hope put down her glass of mineral water and raised a brow. "That's a hot ticket. I've been hinting to Rob for weeks to start looking into reservations so he can take me there for my birthday."

Unless there's a buy-one-get-one-free coupon, good luck with that, I thought, remembering the prices on the menu. As always, I kept my opinions about her cheap fiancé to myself. After all, Rob was going to be family soon.

"And?" Plum prodded.

I shrugged. "It was nice."

"Nice?" Hope threw her hands in the air.

"Is that all you have to say after all the trouble you've gone through to meet this guy? Have you forgot the Delilah-inspired makeover and your ill-advised scrape with that mugger?"

Plum rolled her eyes toward the crown-molding-trimmed ceiling. "Come on, Hope. We both know Riley would have chased down that mugger regardless of whether Mr. Perfect...I mean this Ian she's being so tight-lipped about, was involved."

"I am *not* being tight-lipped! Geez, I had a nice time. What else do you two want me to say?"

The little I actually remembered about my date had been pleasant enough. The food was overrated, but Ian had been as handsome and sophisticated in person as he'd been in my dreams. He'd worn a tailored suit with a pale lavender shirt and coordinating tie. The minor facial injuries he'd suffered during the mugging had already started to fade.

I believe he'd said he was an executive with an ice cream company. To be honest, we were both distracted. Ian's phone had chimed constantly with messages. Even when he silenced it, he kept pulling the vibrating device from his suit jacket pocket to check it.

It hadn't bothered me, though. My body had been at the restaurant picking at the food on my plate and participating in the small talk two strangers make when they are trying to get to know each other. But memories of Hudson Parker had been in my head all evening. His taste. His scent. Images of his hands and mouth all over me had ruled my thoughts.

They still did. Damned Parker had managed to intrude on my first date with my dream man without even being there.

Plum cleared her throat and leaned forward on the sofa. “Since you’re forcing me to play detective, let’s start with that get ’em girl dress. What was his reaction? Did it make his eyes pop out of his head like Delilah guaranteed?”

“He never saw it,” I whispered, diverting my eyes.

“I don’t understand,” Plum said. “We all agreed back at the department store fitting room that it was the perfect date dress.”

My sister huffed out a perturbed sigh. “Riley Sinclair, if you don’t start spilling right this minute, I’m going to join our company softball team.”

Her threat got my attention. Oh, hell no. Hope knew my Achilles heel and wore that prissy smirk of hers as she stomped all over it with her sensible pumps.

“With me on the field, I doubt you’ll ever see that championship trophy again.”

“Okay, okay,” I conceded for the sake of a trophy I hadn’t thought a lick about when it sat just a few feet away from where Parker had me naked against his office wall. “I did wear the dress last night.”

"I'm lost. So why didn't Ian see you in it?" Plum asked.

"Because I took a detour before our date," I answered. "I stopped by Parker Construction's headquarters to give its owner a piece of my mind about those ringers he hired to play on his team. There was a mishap with the dress."

"Oh, Riley." Hope shook her head. "What did you do this time? Attack the poor man like he was that awful mugger, and get your dress dirty?"

"Actually, it ripped."

Hope tsk-tsked me.

"The material was flimsy," I argued.

My sister opened her mouth to start in on me again.

Plum stopped her with a wave of a hand. "Hold that thought, Miss Priss." She stared at me with narrowed eyes. "Yeah, the material was thin all right, but where did it rip exactly?" She reached for her wineglass as she awaited my answer.

"The entire bottom half."

She froze, the wineglass at her lips, and raised a brow. "Were you wearing…?"

"Nope."

I could practically see the gears in her head turning. "So that means you were…?"

"She was what?" Hope asked, looking from one of us to the other.

"Showing my ass in Hudson Parker's office, *literally*."

Revelation dawned in Hope's eyes, and her chin dropped to her chest. Plum burst into a fit of laughter. When it subsided, she hit me with a barrage of questions. "Oh, my God. What did he say? What did you do? What happened?"

"Long story short, Delilah's absolutely right about it being a get 'em girl dress, because I got it all right." There was no use trying to hold out on these two. "Only it wasn't from the man I'd dressed to impress."

"You and Hudson?" Hope asked. Apparently, my words hadn't sunk in.

Plum's face split into a huge grin. "You heard her. Keep up." She turned to me. "So how was it?"

Before I could stop it, my own face split into a grin wider than my friend's. "Good as hell."

Plum's high-pitched squeal filled the room. "And you went on your date with Mr. Perfect afterward?"

I nodded.

"Now *that* is a Delilah Cole *Hot Mess* of a move!" She rose from the sofa and held up her hand in front of me. I slapped it with a high five.

My sister frowned. Confusion still marred her delicate features. "What about all that business about Hudson Parker not being your type?"

Plum harrumphed as she plopped back down on the sofa. "You saw that man," she said. "He's every woman's type."

Hope reached for a second cucumber sandwich, reminding me to hit up McDonald's drive-thru on the way home. "You've always said that you can't stand him."

"I still can't stand him," I explained.

"But..." The word rang out in stereo.

I cut off their protests. "Before you two start jumping to the erroneous conclusion that Parker and I are all booed up, I want to make it clear that sex with him was a one-time deal. I know it. He knows it. No way is he getting in my panties again."

Plum shook her head. "That's a damn shame."

"What panties?" my sister scoffed. "You weren't wearing any!"

I snorted. "Regardless, I'm putting the entire incident in my rearview mirror and focusing on the man I *really* want, Ian King."

Plum shrugged. "For what it's worth, your date with Mr. Perfect sounded pretty dull," she said. "Especially when compared to your pre-date activity with Mr. Construction Boss."

"*I am* a construction boss," I reminded her. My evening with Ian hadn't been exactly dull, just overshadowed by Parker. "Plus, Ian's already asked me for a second date. He's taking me to the opening of a new art exhibit."

Hope refilled her water glass. A

lightweight when it came to alcohol, she provided wine, but rarely indulged. "An art exhibit. You?" she asked, incredulous. "Who's the artist? The guy who paints the pictures of dogs playing poker?"

Plum joined in as my sister laughed at her own joke. My friend caught the scowl tightening my lips. "Come on, Riley. Even you have to admit it's not exactly your style."

They were right, of course. However, if it meant going on another date with Ian, I'd get into it. I was ready to focus entirely on him. "Well, I'm changing my style. That's the whole point of the Delilah Cole app, right?"

Plum took a sip of wine, and then sat the half-empty glass on the coffee table. "Still sounds snoozy," she said. "In your shoes, I'd stop by Hudson Parker's office beforehand for more sexy times."

I shook my head. "The only thing I'd make a second trip to Parker's office for is to personally pick up that trophy after we win the softball championship. If he thinks sexing me is going to keep me from kicking his team's ass, he's wrong."

"Oh, Riley," Hope admonished.

"Now, if you two are done with the inquisition, can we please watch the show?" I took in their skeptical faces. "I've already told y'all, Parker and I were a one-time deal."

"So you've said." Plum grabbed the remote control and aimed it at the television.

If men could hit it and forget it, I could,

too. And I meant it. I wouldn't allow good dick to ruin another evening with the man of my dreams.

The next evening, I stood beside Ian as he studied a painting, pressing my lips together to stifle a yawn. It resulted in a muffled sound that sounded a lot like *hmmm*.

"Yes, it is interesting, isn't it?" My date continued to stare at a landscape the artist had dubbed "Beach in the Moonlight," tossing out the words *angles*, *shading* and *light* in a complimentary fashion. Other people looking at the painting seemed to agree.

I nodded and smiled at the appropriate pauses, simply happy to be on Ian's arm tonight. He looked good. His casual attire of khaki trousers and a short-sleeve, button-down shirt reminded me of ads for designer clothes and cologne featuring men too handsome to be real posing in front of yachts and stately homes. Everything about him was class. From the moment we'd stepped into the gallery located in the city's 12 South neighborhood, he'd drawn the eyes of every woman in the room.

"What do you think, Riley?" he asked.

I blinked as the people surrounding us all looked in my direction. Silently I prayed I wasn't giving off a deer-caught-in-the-headlights vibe, because that's exactly how I felt.

Clearing my throat, I licked my suddenly dry lips. "U-uh, like you said, interesting."

It was unlike me to not call it as I saw it. If I'd been honest, I would have told them that graffiti on the sides of buildings held more appeal than this painting. That went for the rest of this artist's collection, too. I examined the painting again, hoping to catch on to what everyone else saw in it.

Nope. Nothing.

I knew art was subjective, so I tried to keep an open mind. To me, the painting just looked like a mat someone had wiped wet, dirty boots on after coming in from the rain. A kid learning to wield a crayon could have done better.

My date beamed at me. His smile was worth it, so I decided to keep my mouth shut for a change, instead of blurting out exactly what I thought. We ambled away to look at another painting, but that one didn't look any better. Taking my cue from Ian, I accepted a glass of champagne from a server making the rounds.

"Enjoying yourself?" he asked.

I nodded, afraid that if I opened my mouth, another yawn would escape.

"Great." He glanced at the contents of his champagne flute before meeting my gaze. "Honestly, I was hesitant to come here tonight. The artist, Stefanie Miller, is a friend of the family. My mother couldn't make it and insisted I come in her place."

Jazz filtered through hidden speakers, underscoring the buzz of conversation going on around us. Ian leaned in. "In case I haven't mentioned it tonight, you look amazing."

His compliment caught me off guard. I froze as it sunk in, and then a grin exploded across my face. I'd worn a short shift dress in a bold graphic print with strappy sandals. My locs were swept off my face and banded together in a low side ponytail. Ian's approval had affirmed the Delilah app's assertion that using color to stand out in a sea of black dresses at events would appeal to my date.

A man Ian had introduced me to earlier as the owner of the gallery sidled up to us. "I noticed you had your eye on a few of Stefanie's paintings," he said. "I wanted to give you a head's-up that sales have been brisk tonight."

"I'm not surprised," Ian said.

Well, I was certainly taken aback. My dad used to say that you could put a price tag on a turd and someone would buy it. I'd always thought it was a joke, but it turned out he was right.

The gallery owner slapped Ian on the back. "Well, if there was something you wanted in particular, I suggest you make a move on it quickly."

I pressed my lips together to stop myself from interjecting as I watched Ian reach into his pocket for what I assumed was his credit card. Instead, he pulled out his phone. He glanced at the flashing screen, and a frown creased his perfect features.

"It's a business call. Do you mind?"

"Not at all. It'll give me an opportunity to visit the ladies' room and touch up my lipstick." In reality, the lacy thong panties Delilah had suggested wearing in lieu of going commando felt like they were slicing my ass in half.

I walked through a lounge area with pink suede armchairs that reminded me of Hope's condo to the bathroom. Moments later, I stood at the vanity checking my makeup. I'd spent the majority of the evening with my lips fused together in order to keep my opinion to myself. Still, they could use another coat of gloss. I was trying to free the lip color from my tiny purse when I heard a strident, pissed-off female voice coming from the lounge.

"I cannot believe Ian brought a date to my opening after all the plotting me and his mother did to make sure he showed up," she said. "He's always so caught up in work, neither of us considered he'd actually bring someone."

"But look at her, Stef." Another woman's voice chimed in. "The woman's average at best. In your shoes, I wouldn't consider her competition."

"But *she's* the one on his arm." Although we hadn't met yet, I assumed it was Stefanie Miller who was talking. I could hear the pout in her voice. "Tonight was supposed to be about me, my art, and making an impression on Ian King, but he hasn't pulled himself away from that big-boned chick long enough to even say hello."

Big-boned? Humph.

I heard the creak of the door opening and another person enter the lounge area. Now would have been the perfect opportunity to step out and reveal my presence. Some folks, my sister for instance, would have called my eavesdropping impolite. The way I saw it, gossiping was the bigger etiquette crime, and those women shouldn't be saying anything aloud they didn't want to risk being overheard.

A memory of the last time I'd overheard something not meant for my ears popped into my head.

"One night in my bed, and Riley Sinclair will be up the next morning cooking breakfast, wearing nothing but an apron, high heels, and a satisfied smile."

I caught a glimpse of my flushed face in the mirror as Hudson Parker's words echoed through my mind. An hour pinned between him and his office wall had proven the notion wasn't as preposterous as I'd initially thought.

Oh, my, that man could kiss, and good lawd, he certainly knew how to... *No. No. No. No.* I put the brakes on the onslaught of illicit images flooding my brain. Dammit, I refused to allow Parker to encroach upon another evening.

"Honey, let me give you the lowdown on Ian's date." The voice of one of the women in the lounge drew me out of my reverie.

"What about her?" Stefanie Miller asked.

Yeah, what about me? Ian and I had talked briefly to a lot of people tonight, but I couldn't imagine any of them having the so-called *lowdown* on me.

"Well, when Ian introduced her to me and Brad, he mentioned that she'd chased down the guy who had mugged him and got his stolen stuff back."

I heard a huff that sounded like it came from Stefanie. "So now she's a hero, too. Great. I thought you were going to tell me something that would make me feel better."

"Don't you see?" her friend asked. "All Ian is feeling toward her is gratitude. Once he gets past it, I can't imagine her holding much appeal. I mean, she's cute in a common kind of way, but nothing like the gorgeous women he's usually with. She can't touch you in the looks department."

Gratitude. Now *that* stung. Then again, I'd thought the same thing when Ian had asked me out, and he'd immediately nixed the notion.

Stefanie giggled. "I guess you're right. Besides, did y'all see her arms? I think Ian's date has bigger muscles than he does."

Their laughter filled both rooms. Staring in the vanity mirror, I checked out my bare arms in the sleeveless shift. I flexed a bicep and nodded in approval at my reflection. No, I didn't have their Pilates-honed forms. My muscles came from long days of hard work, and nothing or no one would ever make me ashamed of them.

Besides, their cattiness had begun to bore me. Three surprised faces greeted me as I stepped into the lounge area.

"Evening, ladies." Although my sister and Plum called me rude, I was still a girl who'd been raised in the South. Greetings came natural.

The woman of the hour was the first to recover from my sudden appearance. "I guess you heard us," Stefanie raised a defiant brow.

"Every word." Leveling a gaze at the three of them, I couldn't help grinning.

The one who thought she was giving her friends the supposed scoop on my relationship with Ian spoke up. "Then why are you smiling?"

"Because thanks to you ladies, I now have something I've never had before: *haters*."

Back in school, I'd never had any run ins with gossiping mean-girl cliques. They were too afraid of me kicking their asses, and I probably would have. Besides, all I did back then was count the seconds until my last class and get my homework done so I could shadow my father around construction sites.

"Now if y'all will excuse me, I'm gonna have to shake you off and enjoy my date." I sauntered past the lounge clique, and returned to the main room of the gallery just in time. Ian had wrapped up the call he'd taken outside and had been looking for me.

"Sorry for leaving you," Ian said. "I'm even sorrier we haven't had much time to talk tonight."

"No worries."

He rested a hand on the small of my back and leaned in. "I was thinking I could introduce you to Stefanie, and then we can get out of here. Maybe grab some coffee and talk."

"Sounds good. Oh, I've already had the pleasure of meeting Stefanie."

He flashed that perfect smile. It looked even better up close and directed at me. "Great." Ian glanced around the room. "I was going to say good night, but I don't see her anywhere. Looks like this evening was a big success for her, so I doubt she'll even notice we've left."

I nodded in agreement. As we turned to leave, I caught a glimpse of the artist glaring at me from across the room. Hope would have been proud of me, because somehow I resisted the urge to stick my tongue out. This wasn't sports, and there was no need for me to rub in the fact that I was clearly the winner. It was enough that I was leaving with the man she'd expected would be hers for the night.

CHAPTER 13

HUDSON

Light from the kitchen window illuminated the darkness as I paced my backyard to cool down from an early-morning run. I preferred working out before dawn, when most folks were still in bed. It allowed me to clear my head of old business and focus on the day ahead. Only it hadn't worked so well lately.

Last week's sexcapade with Riley in my office should've been old business by now. She'd made it clear we were a one-and-done deal, only now I wanted more. I just needed to come up with a plan to put our deal up for renegotiation.

The aroma of coffee greeted me inside the house. That didn't surprise me; the coffeemaker was on timer. What I didn't expect was to see my sister sitting at the kitchen table.

"You're up early," I said, accustomed to

both her and my niece still asleep in one of the spare rooms when I left for work.

Caryn shrugged. "Couldn't sleep."

Taking in her defeated expression, I washed my hands, pulled two mugs from the cabinet, and I filled one with coffee. I poured milk into the other and slid it in front of my sister.

"Need to talk?" I leaned against the counter facing the table.

She stared into the contents of her mug. "Yesterday was my birthday," she said softly.

I glanced at my smartwatch, which had been craftily hidden beneath Fee's stuffed animal menagerie. The date flashed up at me along with my heart rate, the time, and the current temperature. *Damn.* I immediately wished her a happy belated birthday. "Sorry, it totally slipped my mind."

My sister looked up from her mug. "You weren't the only one. I thought for sure Will would reach out, but not a peep."

Caryn didn't ask for my opinion, and I didn't offer it. She got enough of that from our mother. Regardless of any mistakes my sister may or may not have made, she wasn't stupid. I was confident she'd come to any realizations or solutions on her own.

In the meantime, she looked so dejected that the big brother in me couldn't help wanting to do something to lift her spirits, something that didn't include handing over my credit card for her to throw another party for her friends on my dime.

"How about we go out for dinner tomorrow night?"

"You don't have to do that, Hudson."

Walking over to the table, I nudged her shoulder with my elbow. "I have tickets to see that comedian from the cop-buddy comedies you like so much. You can ask one of your sorority sisters to watch Fee, and we'll make a night of it."

"I wouldn't be very good company," she said. "Besides, I'm sure there are plenty of women you'd rather take out than your pesky baby sister."

Actually, I'd had intended to ask Riley, but I figured convincing her to go on an actual date with me was going to be a lot tougher than getting her out of her clothes, which thanks to her dress ripping, had practically been a gimme.

Nudging my sister again, I sweetened the pot. "I'll even spring for dessert: triple-chocolate cake."

She forced a half smile that I suspected was just for my sake. "Okay," she finally agreed. This time her smile was a little more genuine. "You know I'm not one to turn down cake, especially one with three kinds of chocolate."

"Good." I grabbed two strawberry cereal bars from a box in the cabinet and tossed her one.

She peeled open the wrapper and took a

bite. “This is an early hour, even for you. What’s up with the suit hanging on the door of the front hall closet? Wedding or funeral?”

“Neither.” I dunked my cereal bar in my coffee, before demolishing it in two bites.

Caryn screwed up her face like she used to do when she was a kid. “Ew.”

“I have an interview for a big job I’m bidding on. The city’s narrowed it down to three companies.” I glanced at my watch. My interview at the mayor’s office wasn’t for hours yet, but I wanted to check on the hotel we’d broken ground on earlier in the month and stop by my own office. I could change into my suit there.

“Must be huge for you to break out a suit and tie.” She nibbled at the cereal bar.

I nodded. “Opportunities like this are why I uprooted Parker Construction from Atlanta to move here.” I also intended to do everything in my power to make a good impression and get this contract.

“Good luck.” Caryn drained her mug of milk.

The sound of small feet slapping the hardwood floors preceded the appearance of my niece, who was wearing purple pajamas emblazoned with the smiling face of a cartoon doctor. Her sleepy eyes lit up at the sight of me, and she ran past her mother and held up her arms for me to pick her up. I hoisted her into my arms and planted a kiss on her chubby cheek.

"How's my favorite girl doing this morning?" I asked.

She giggled in response and rested her head on my chest.

Caryn looked at her daughter and sucked her teeth in faux annoyance. "That's kids for you. No loyalty."

"Can I help it if I'm charming and irresistible to women of all ages?" I tickled my niece's tummy. "Isn't that right, Fee?"

Fiona bobbed her head in agreement while my sister rolled her eyes. "For some reason I can't fathom, my single friends in town are all nagging me to hook them up with you," she said. "Speaking of which…"

"Not interested." Time to shut down that idea before it took hold and I came home to find myself ambushed by one of my sister's high-maintenance line sisters on a husband hunt. "Besides, I already have my hands full with this little lady." I looked over the top of my niece's head full of coily hair and smiled. "She reminds me of you at this age."

"That's what Mom said." Caryn zeroed in on her daughter. "In fact, she said Fiona was becoming *too much like me*."

I looked at my sister quizzically and was on the brink of asking her to elaborate when my niece lifted her head off my chest. "I want cookies. Now!"

"No, ma'am," Caryn interjected sternly. "It's too early in the morning for cookies."

"Please…" Fiona exaggerated the word.

"No," my sister repeated firmly.

The grin on Fiona's cherub face morphed into a pout, but it didn't last long. She grasped my face between her chubby palms. "Cookies. Cookies. Cookies."

How could I refuse? I pulled two Oreos from the jar on the counter, handed one to my niece and took a bite out of the other. The kid held the cookie in her outstretched hand.

For a split second it looked like she was taunting her mother with the fact she possessed the forbidden treat before she popped it into her mouth. But that was ridiculous. She was just a baby. Sure, the kid had sticky fingers when it came to my electronic gadgets, but she didn't have a cunning bone in her body.

"She did say *please.*" I defended my actions, but my sister wasn't looking at me. She was staring at her daughter, a strange expression on her face.

Caryn mumbled something mostly unintelligible. I could only make out the words Mom and right. I thought I must have heard her wrong, because my mother and sister hadn't seen eye to eye in years.

"Down, please," Fiona directed.

I put my niece's feet on the floor and smiled as she scampered out of the kitchen. My sister rose from the table, opened the refrigerator and refilled her mug. I helped myself to another Oreo.

"You're not pissed about the cookie, are

you? I tried not to give in, but who could resist that little face?"

Caryn shrugged. "I'm beginning to think it might be more my fault than yours." Standing beside me at the counter, she sipped her milk. "FYI, she swiped your watch."

I glanced at my empty wrist. "Damn, she got me again."

"Sucker," Caryn chuckled.

"Fee!" I shouted, and took off down the hallway after my niece.

CHAPTER 14

RILEY

My thumb hovered over the disconnect button on the touch screen, and I made a hissing noise that hopefully sounded like static. "You're breaking up, Hope."

"This connection is clear as a bell. Don't you dare hang up on me, Riley!"

"You're driving me nuts." I made two laps around my living room and dining room in search of my keys, only to discover they were in my other hand.

Today was the big interview for a job we'd bid on with the city, and with our mother still out of the country, I'd be representing Sinclair Construction in her place. Mom and I had worked together on the initial proposal, so I knew the particulars as well as she did.

Nerves weren't a factor—until Hope had started in on me first thing this morning. She rattled off a string of questions she damn well already knew the answers to.

"Are you sure you don't want to take this meeting instead of me?"

"Of course not. I have a full schedule at the office. Besides, we both know in Mom's absence, you're the best person to handle it," Hope said.

"Well, in that case, shut your piehole and let me get ready."

My sister pressed on as if she hadn't heard. "You aren't wearing your work clothes downtown, are you? Maybe I should stop by your place on my way to work."

"No, and no." I glared at the phone.

"Well, what are you wearing then?"

"You sound like a perv calling a phone-sex line."

I placed the phone on the console table near my front entrance and put my tablet computer into my tote bag. A quick glance in the mirror confirmed my appearance was professional enough, despite Hope's doubts.

My locs were corralled into a low bun at the base of my neck, just the way Ian preferred them. I wore a sleeveless navy shift dress, a multicolored scarf, and sky-high heels. All purchases from my Delilah Cole–inspired shopping spree. Her app had called it the "perfect business ensemble."

Still, Hope continued to rail in my ear. "And for goodness sake, make sure you put some underwear on. The last thing we need is for you to go show your behind in the mayor's office, the way you did over at Parker Construction."

"Okay, I'm hanging up now."

My sister was still talking when I swiped the screen to end the call. I felt the sudden surge of heat as it warmed every spot on my body that Hudson Parker had touched, kissed, and licked that day in his office. *Sigh.* Every time I thought I'd successfully relegated the interlude to the recesses of my mind, the images returned full force.

Just stop, I silently admonished my wayward thoughts. It was Ian I should be thinking, not Parker.

"So what if he's a good kisser?" I muttered. "He's still an ass." Damn. The word roused even more pictures in my mind. "Well, so what if he can kiss and has an incredible rear view?" I amended.

An incoming text chimed on my phone. It was Ian asking if I was free for dinner tomorrow night. We'd been out nearly every night since the art gallery. I tapped out a quick reply, making it a date.

I liked Ian. He was smart, polished, and extremely easy on the eye. So what if his kisses didn't melt me the way Parker's had? They would eventually; I just had to give it more time, because despite my traitorous mind and body, *Ian was the man I wanted.*

My phone chimed again. Seeing Hope's name on the screen reminded me that now wasn't the time to be thinking about men.

Sinclair Construction had to be my main focus this morning. Landing this contract was huge.

I gathered my things, including jeans and work boots to change into later. The interview wasn't for over an hour yet, but with Nashville's increasing traffic problem, I wanted to give myself plenty of time.

Stepping onto the carport, I briefly considered Hope's suggestion about driving my sedan instead of the vehicle she referred to as *that raggedy pickup.* Like most of her advice, I simply disregarded it. I slung my things onto the passenger seat of my truck. I had a job to go to after I left the mayor's office, and I didn't want to return home to switch vehicles.

Twenty minutes later, I was still inching my truck through traffic. Both interstates leading into downtown were backed up with fender benders and the effects of commuting in a rapidly growing city with a population of nearly two million people. A check of my phone's GPS revealed it was also slow going on side streets. All I could do was wait for a break in traffic to make up for lost time.

That break finally came at that point in the road where rubberneckers had gotten their fill gawking at an overturned car on the side of the highway and started driving again. I could see the downtown skyline in the distance, including the cranes looming over Sinclair Construction projects in progress.

Just as I was about to floor it, my truck suddenly jerked and then slowed. Next came the dreaded sound of rubber flapping against asphalt. *Damn.* Nobody ever needed a flat tire, but I especially didn't need one now. Not with a multimillion-dollar job at stake. Luckily there was an exit just a few yards ahead, so I didn't have to risk pulling over onto the shoulder to change it.

A few minutes later, I parked on the first street off the expressway, threw open the driver-side door and stepped out of the truck. I tried to be as ladylike as possible in heels as I surveyed the damage. My right rear tire was flat as a pancake. Exhaling, I quickly debated calling Hope or someone from my work crew to give me a lift downtown, but I knew I could put on the spare in the time it would take for either to show up. There was no way could I show up late for this meeting.

I leaned inside the cab to retrieve the key from the ignition and grab the pickup's changing kit. Donning my work gloves, I unlocked the spare beneath the truck bed and used the rods from the changing kit to lower it to the ground.

Holding the jack in my hands, I hesitated. This was a first. I'd changed plenty of tires, but I'd never had to worry about my clothes until now. I glanced down at my Delilah Cole-approved outfit and frowned. There was no avoiding having to get on the ground to place the jack. Damn. I yanked my pink work boots from the truck bed and fished around for something to shield my dress from the pavement.

Another truck caught my attention as it slowed and then parked in front of mine. I'd seen the black pickup before, as well as the logo on its passenger-side door. *Parker Construction.*

Maybe it was just a truck from Parker's company fleet. It didn't necessarily have to be him, I reasoned, as I stared at its brake lights. I hadn't seen Parker since that day in his office, and my emotions ricocheted somewhere between dread and spine-tingling anticipation.

The pickup's door swung open, and I watched the driver step out. It was Parker all right, but not the version of him I was accustomed to seeing. He wore a navy suit and a crisp white shirt that highlighted the rich coffee tones of his dark skin. The morning sun glinted off the gold rims of his aviator sunglasses as he strode toward me.

Good Lawd.

Even I had to admit the man could wear the hell out of a business suit. Goosebumps erupted on my arms, and the parts of my body that had warmed at the mere thought of him earlier were now downright hot.

He's not your type. The silent admonishment was no match for the woman in me that was so glad to see him. But it was something I needed to squash ASAP. Sex with Parker was one thing; falling for him was something else. I refused to let it happen.

He greeted me with a quick nod and inclined his head toward my pickup. "Trouble?"

His clean-shaven face was impassive. The mirror lenses of his shades shielded his dark eyes from my scrutiny and robbed me of the ability to get a read on what he was thinking.

"It's just a flat." Jack in hand, I walked around to the side of the truck with the damaged tire.

"From the way you're dressed, I'm assuming we're headed to the same place." He rested his hand on the rim of the truck bed. "City hall, right?"

"Yep." The question cemented the fact that he wasn't a man I should be lusting after and screwing against office walls. He was the competition.

"I'd heard Sinclair was one of the top three candidates for this project." Parker glanced at his bare wrist as if he were wearing a watch, frowned, and shook his head. "Look, you can ride with me. I'll bring you back to your truck after our interviews."

I blinked as his offer caught me off guard. "You'd do that knowing we're both after the same job?"

He removed his sunglasses and leveled me

with his dark-eyed gaze. "Yeah, I would."

Three simple words, but he delivered them in a way that felt genuine, as if he really cared about me. The memory of Parker's other reply, when I'd asked him what the hell he thought he was doing seconds before he'd kissed me, popped into my head.

What I want to do every time I see you.

A lump of emotion rose to my throat as I stared up at him, and I swallowed, hard. My common sense battled with the deep-down part of me that could easily get caught up in him. It also reminded me that I had too much at stake this morning. I couldn't let Parker get into my head or allow memories of good dick to throw me off my game.

I cleared my throat. "No thanks."

"For goodness sake! Why not?"

"I don't need anything from you, Parker."

"We're talking about a ten-minute ride. What's the big deal?"

"The big deal is we aren't friendly. We aren't friends. I don't even like you." My rant sounded pretty ridiculous, even to me, considering what I'd already done with him.

He raised a brow. "You don't like me, or you're just too damn scared to face the fact that you already do?"

The question hung in the air, waiting for the deep-down part of me to answer. I tried to dismiss it, but my silence spoke volumes.

Parker shook his head. "Just forget it."

I knew he was pissed, and I expected him

to stalk back to his truck and take off. Instead, he surprised me by shedding his suit jacket and draping it across the rim of my truck's bed. Then he began rolling up his shirtsleeves.

"What are you doing?"

It was his turn to ignore a question. He took the jack from my hand.

"I can do it myself." I tried to snatch it back from his grip, but he held it just out of my reach.

He grunted. "I know you can." His intense gaze zeroed in on me. "It's one of the things I admire most about you, when you're not being such a stubborn ass."

Admire? He had surprised me again, making it harder and harder to remember the reasons why I couldn't stand him.

"Why?" I blurted out, grasping for an ulterior motive on his part. "On today of all days, with so much at stake, why would you want to help me?"

"Because any man who is worth a damn would."

CHAPTER 15

RILEY

The next evening I stared across the table at Ian, trying to etch his perfect features into my brain. I hoped that if I looked at him long enough, his face would overtake any renegade thoughts of Parker. I simply couldn't get the man off my mind, no matter how hard I tried.

Memories of our time together in his office had been bad enough. Now he'd gone and compounded them by being a damn gentleman. Changing a flat tire wasn't a big deal; I'd done it countless times myself. However, it became a huge deal when a man takes the time to do it on the way to an interview for an extremely lucrative job. One you're both competing to get.

Don't like me, or just too damn scared to face the fact that you already do?

"Riley?" Ian covered my hand with his.

"Everything okay?"

I nodded.

"You sure? Because you've seemed distracted all through dinner."

"It's nothing. I'm fine."

Our waiter cleared our dinner plates and presented us with dessert menus. I opened mine and immediately began browsing the downtown Italian restaurant's offerings. It wasn't like I could admit to Ian that I'd spent the majority of our date preoccupied with another man.

Ian looked over the top of his menu. "Oh, I forgot to ask earlier. How did yesterday's meeting with the mayor go?"

"Good. She seemed impressed with what I had to say. In fact, I'm cautiously optimistic about Sinclair Construction's chances of landing this one."

"That's great."

Silence ensued, and not because we were absorbed in the dessert menu. It was an awkward kind of silence: the kind that happened when two people had exhausted their repertoire of small talk and struggled to find something else to say. Fortunately, the waiter reappeared quickly to take our orders. Ian requested the wild berry tart while I opted for triple-chocolate cake.

"So what did you think of the symphony tonight?" Ian asked.

I thought whoever had come up with the idea for the city's symphony orchestra to cover the top twenty-five rap hits of all time needed their ass kicked. "Truly unforgettable."

That much was true. It would be a long time before I could forget the strains of my favorite rapper Wangs' iconic hit "2-piece" played on violin and cello, with none of the thumping bass that had kept it number one on the music charts for over a year.

Ian beamed. "I knew you'd enjoy it."

The table fell silent again.

"Oh, did you hear that the Titans are considering..."

He shook his head just as I remembered he wasn't a sports fan. His face drew a blank whenever I talked about softball. Ian only followed pro cycling, which I honestly didn't even consider a sport. Then he went on to talk about the winner of the Tour de France.

Swallowing a yawn, I nodded and smiled as I often did during our conversations. It was something my friends would have called me out on. But the way I saw it, Ian King wasn't just any man. He was the Mr. Perfect I'd knocked myself out to meet. Now that we were actually dating, so what if I had to make a few compromises.

I looked up and spotted a familiar figure being led to a table behind Ian, right in my line of sight.

Parker.

And he wasn't alone. My eyeballs burned holes in his broad back as he held out the chair for a diminutive slip of a woman. The type most men found preferable to my sturdy, thick frame. Her hair fell past her slim shoulders in silky waves. I felt my stomach do a free fall as she smiled up at him with adoring eyes. Hell, the woman was stunning. I had to wonder: if Parker was seeing someone this gorgeous, what was he playing at with me?

"Riley?" Ian called my name.

"What?" I barked, then caught my date's surprised expression and quickly apologized. "Um, you startled me."

"The waiter asked if you wanted regular or decaf coffee. He's been waiting on your answer."

I ordered the regular coffee extra strong as I shot another look past Ian at Parker and his date.

"Are you sure there isn't something bothering you?"

"No, of course not." I kept my eyes trained on my date, determined not to let Parker's presence spoil our evening.

Satisfied with my answer, Ian nodded. "Well, there is something I wanted to talk to you about."

I bobbed my head once for him to continue, hoping whatever he had to say would take my mind off the man seated a few tables away.

"The Labor Day holiday is coming up in a few weeks, and if you don't already have plans, I'd like to take you on a romantic getaway for the three-day weekend," he said. "I was thinking about New York City. We can take in the sights and spend some *real time together.*"

Ian's emphasis on the last few words, combined with the look in his light-brown eyes, told me the proposed weekend would be about taking our relationship to the next level. He obviously wanted more than the pleasant kisses we'd shared at the end of our dates. I blinked in surprise. Not at the fact that he was suggesting it, but that sex with him hadn't even crossed my mind.

Oh, it's been on your mind all right.

My gaze involuntarily drifted past Ian to Parker and his date. The woman was laughing so hard at something he'd said she was wiping away tears. Humph. Nothing he had to say could be *that* funny.

Ian cleared his throat. Shit, he'd just asked me about going away with him, and here I was gawking at stupid Parker.

The waiter saved me by picking that exact moment to return with our coffee and dessert. Get it together, Riley, I silently scolded myself as he placed the hunk of chocolate cake in front of me. What Hudson Parker does, and whomever he does it with, is none of your business. Especially when your dream man wants to take you on a romantic weekender.

I looked up at Ian's expectant face, and

then I suddenly remembered the championship softball game was the Friday evening of the long weekend. I fully expected our team to be playing in that game.

"This game stuff is a big deal to you, so I guess you can't give it a miss," he said after I'd explained the situation.

The answer to that was *hell no.* I would have told anyone that straight out. However, for Ian, my Mr. Perfect, I smiled demurely and shook my head.

"How about we leave early Saturday morning instead? That still gives us plenty of time to visit a museum or two, and take in a Broadway show."

"Or a Yankees or a Mets game," I blurted out excitedly. But then I remembered he wasn't into sports. "Or maybe not." Regardless, this trip would be a great way to celebrate bringing the softball league championship back to Sinclair Construction after we won the game.

I cut into the slab of cake with my fork and took a huge bite. Then I noticed Ian hadn't touched his tart.

He picked up his fork, but it hovered over his dessert as he looked up at me. "There was something else…" His voice trailed off.

"What's up?"

"I like you, Riley. I like you a lot." He finally took a bite of his tart and chewed slowly, as if he were measuring his next words. "As much as I'm looking forward to whisking you away for a few days, I don't want there to be any misunderstanding between us."

My gaze shifted to my rival's table as I waited for Ian to tell me what was on his mind. Part of me wanted to march over to Parker, pull up a chair, and tell him off.

For what? Being out on a date, the same as you?

Ian sighed. "Look, I don't mean to sound arrogant, but I've had problems in the past with women reading too much into things too quickly," he said. "I enjoy spending time with you, but at this point in our relationship, we're just having fun getting to know each other. We aren't exclusive, and we're free to see anyone else we please."

"I never thought otherwise." Sure, I'd been crushing on him for weeks, and I hoped wedding bells were in my future, *eventually*. But I hadn't really thought about our relationship beyond dating.

"So you're good with it?"

"Definitely."

Ian reached for his coffee cup, and then paused and went for the inside pocket of his suit jacket instead. I'd been out with him enough times to know his phone had vibrated. I also knew it was work, and he'd more than likely want to take the call.

"Go ahead," I said, forestalling his asking first.

"Thanks." Seconds later, he was deep in

conversation and walking toward the restaurant entrance.

As was starting to become customary when Ian had to take a business call, I headed to the restroom to check my lipstick. The trouble with wearing it all the time now was making sure it was on my lips where it belonged, instead of my teeth.

Minutes later, I emerged to find Parker leaning against the wall across from the restroom. “What do you want?” I asked.

Not bothering to answer, he closed the space between us with one step, pulled me into his arms, and kissed me.

No. No. No. My common sense silently repeated my rejection to those incredibly soft lips, but my traitorous body shouted hell, yeah. I settled into his embrace and fisted my hands in his shirt. In other words, I practically inhaled him.

When we finally came up for air, our gazes collided and held. “Missed me, huh?” The corner of his mouth twitched upward into a half smile.

Snorting, I pushed my hands against his hard chest, unsure what annoyed me most: his arrogance, the fact he was right, or that he was out with another woman.

He wrapped a hand around my arm. “Don’t go.”

I shrugged off his hand. “I have to get back to my date.”

He raised a brow. “It appears to me that

your date is more interested in his phone right now."

Hands on hips, I glared up at him. "And yours?"

"What?"

"The former sorority princess at your table flashing you adoring looks and laughing at every word that comes out of your stupid mouth. If you're gone much longer, she's gonna think you're back here taking a dump."

Parker laughed. As always, I didn't hold back when I talked to him, and he remained unaffected by my crudeness.

"I don't believe it." An easy smile spread over his lips. It reached his eyes and lit up his entire face. He touched his finger to my chest. "You're jealous."

"I am *not* jealous!" The words came out more forcefully than I had intended, earning me the stink-eye from two women about to walk into the ladies' room.

Grabbing my hand, Parker used his free one to push open a door to a room behind us. Then he pulled me inside. The dimly lit room was filled with neatly stacked boxes, which barely left enough room for the two of us. Still holding my hand, he tugged me closer and kissed me again.

It was soft and sweet. I allowed myself a few moments to enjoy it before reluctantly pulling back. I shook my head as if the motion would clear it. "I don't know that woman sitting out there waiting on you, but I won't do this to her. Go back to your date, Parker."

He squeezed my hand. "She can wait."

I snatched my hand away. "You really are an ass."

"She's my sister, Riley. Her name is Caryn."

"S-sister?" I stammered over the word. I shouldn't feel so relieved and giddy.

He nodded. "So you see? You don't have any reason to be jealous."

"How many times do I have to tell you? I'm not jealous. I couldn't care less who you go out with." Sigh. I wasn't much of a liar, and it showed.

Parker smoothed his knuckles down my cheek. "Prove it. Go out with me this Saturday."

"Me, go out with you?" I laughed.

"Yeah, on an honest-to-goodness date," he said. "Unless you're scared of falling for me."

"I won't."

He smiled. "Then I'll see you Saturday."

"Fine, if that's what it takes to get it through your head that I'm not interested." I huffed out a sigh. "Now can I go back to my date?"

"That depends." He stroked the shadow of beard along his jaw that had grown in since I'd seen him yesterday. "Are you wearing panties underneath that pretty dress?"

My mind went back to that scene in his

office, and from the look in Parker's eyes, his had gone there, too. "Yeah, ever since my wardrobe malfunction, I don't leave home without them."

"Good. Just make sure that pretty boy in the suit keeps his hands to himself this evening, because what's in them is all mine."

I snorted, fighting a ridiculous urge to grin. "You wish."

CHAPTER 16

HUDSON

"This date you've planned doesn't sound very romantic," Caryn said. "From the way you were eyeballing her all through dinner the other night, I'd assumed you wanted to impress this woman."

My sister's questioning tone when I'd told her my plans had me second-guessing my choice as I drove over to Riley's place on Saturday. Caryn had suggested scrapping my itinerary entirely and replacing it with lunch at one of the eclectic fusion eateries that were popping up all over town, and then taking in the latest big-screen romantic comedy.

While her idea had sounded fine, there was nothing particularly special about it, and this date needed to be extraordinary. I wanted to give Riley a memory that she wouldn't easily forget.

"Or maybe a spa day with his-and-her massages, facials and pedis!" my sister had squealed, clasping her hands together.

I'd grunted at the suggestion. "I want to be her man, not her girlfriend."

My sister had simply wagged a finger at me. "Don't discount the allure of a metrosexual man. Meticulous grooming is in," she said. "Case and point would be that guy she was with at the restaurant. *Very sexy.*"

Caryn and her husband could spend the day painting each other's toenails for all I cared. Anything to get them back together. I was cool with my Gillette razor and a weekly trip to the barbershop. I couldn't be more different than the guy at Riley's table that night. If that was the kind of man she wanted, then I truly didn't have a chance.

If she was so into him, then she wouldn't have been kissing me.

The thought buoyed me as I parked in front of the house at the address Riley had given me. I'd gone with Caryn's advice to drive my SUV instead of my pickup. Glancing at the gold medallion I'd draped over the rearview mirror earlier, I hoped I was right in going with my gut on everything else.

"I thought we'd have lunch first."

Holding open the passenger-side door, I inhaled the faint scent of Riley's floral-laced fragrance as she climbed in. She'd dressed casually as I'd requested, and although I'd seen Riley in jeans and sneakers plenty of times, this was different.

My hands itched to touch the curves hugged by the figure-flattering denim and fitted tee. I wanted to sink my fingers into the thick locs she'd worn down, just the way I liked, and kiss her until the only thing that came out of that sassy, pink-glossed mouth of hers was my name.

Unfortunately, neither of those things were on my agenda. I closed the door behind her, rounded the SUV, and slid into the driver's seat. This afternoon was all about helping her realize what I already knew—that what she felt for me went deeper than the sexual attraction she tried so hard to ignore.

"Glad to hear I'm getting a free meal out of this date business," Riley said as I started the engine and pulled away from the curb.

"You'll want to eat hearty. You'll need your strength for what I have planned."

"The only reason I agreed to this date was to prove you wrong. I won't need my strength, because you won't be nailing me against your office wall or anywhere else today."

She had it all wrong. I grunted and repeated the line she'd used on me the other night. "You wish."

It got a laugh out of her. I liked the sound of it, but then again, I liked most of what I knew about Riley Sinclair.

I switched on the radio, and a hip-hop track filled the SUV's interior. The lyrics were usually lost on me. I was a grown-assed man well into my thirties, so unless they were rapping about getting up at the crack of dawn, grabbing a lunch pail and heading to work, I couldn't relate. That didn't keep me from enjoying the music's high energy and thumping beat, though.

"You can change the station to whatever you like," I said, remembering my manners.

"It's fine. I listen to the same station all the time."

"Really?" My ex had said the same thing when we were going out. Similar to her professed love of sports, a few weeks after our splashy wedding, I discovered she couldn't stand rap, hip-hop, or much else I'd believed we had in common.

I glanced quickly at Riley. She was bobbing her head in time with the song. I felt my body slowly relax. This woman didn't have to play games to land a man. With her, it was what you see is what you get.

Conversation came easy for us. We instinctively steered clear of two topics—the contract for the city project, and the fact that after our wins this week, we'd be facing each other in the upcoming championship softball game.

"That's one of the dumbest things I've heard," Riley said, incredulous. "Your favorite color can't be *black*."

"Why not?"

"Because black isn't even a color. It's black."

I glanced at her. "What's yours?"

"Blue."

"My guess would have been pink."

I caught her frown out the corner of my eye. She lifted her legs and looked down at her pink Converse sneakers. "Wanted blue, but that stupid app..." she muttered. "My feet look like I'm wearing wads of bubblegum."

"What app?"

"Never mind." She waved off the question. "Favorite food?"

"Pizza." We both said simultaneously, and she elbowed my side. "Maybe you're not all bad, Parker."

"What? Is that a compliment?"

She held up her hand, displaying an inch of space between her thumb and forefinger. "A very small one," she conceded, but there was a smile wrapped in her grudging tone.

"Favorite dessert?"

"That's easy, cake pops."

"Cake, what?"

"Don't tell me you never heard of cake pops."

"Nope."

"Where do you live, under a rock? Think of a lollypop, but instead of candy, it's a perfect bite-size piece of cake."

"Wouldn't it be simpler just to have a slice of cake?"

"Then it wouldn't be a cake pop."

"So how many of these pops do you usually eat in one sitting?"

"I'm not sure. Ten, maybe a dozen?"

"Exactly." Inclining my head in her direction, I got off the expressway and continued to drive south of the city. "Easier just to eat it by the slice."

Riley reached out and touched the gold medallion. "What's this? Parker Construction competing in the Olympics now?"

"Actually, if you're up to the challenge, it could be yours at the end of this date."

"Huh?"

"I'll explain it to you over lunch."

Shortly afterward we were seated at my favorite barbecue joint. I'd eaten nearly half of a smoked turkey sandwich, and Riley was demolishing a salad heaped with so much meat you could barely make out the tomatoes and leafy greens.

"I'd ask if your food was good, but I don't think you've put that fork down or looked up from your plate once."

She finally pulled her head out of her meal. Reaching for her sweet tea, she eyed me over the rim of the glass as she drank. "This salad is fantastic," she finally said. "Now I want to hear more about the gold medal in your truck, and what it has to do with our date."

I wiped my hands with a paper napkin, and began to fill her in on the details of the date I couldn't imagine taking any woman on but her. My hope had been it would appeal to her competitive nature, and the sparkle in Riley's eyes as she listened confirmed I was on the right track.

"So let me get this straight," she said. "We're going to race go-carts, play miniature golf, and shoot baskets at the arcade and bowl."

I raised a finger to interject. "Not play, *compete*. We're going head-to-head in the four activities, and at the end, the winner will take home the gold."

Leaning forward, I lowered my voice and infused it with a taunting tone. "That is, if you aren't afraid of getting your ass kicked."

She narrowed her eyes in that cute way only Riley could do. I couldn't resist continuing to press her buttons, in the way only I could do. "Since I already have two championship trophies sitting in my office, naturally you'd be scared of getting that pretty ass of yours beat by me *yet again*."

I leaned back in my chair and grinned at her scowling face. Riley opened her mouth as if she were about to tear me a new one. Then she closed it, only to open it and snap it shut again. She inclined her head, and a slow, not-so-sweet smile spread over her lips.

"Game on, Parker."

If Riley was a sore loser, she was an even worse winner.

"I *won*!" she yelled. Her shout was loud enough to wake the occupants of the cemetery a mile down the road from the family fun center where the go-karts, arcade, and miniature golf course were located.

"W-o-n!" She spelled the word out like I was slow, and then jabbed a finger into my chest. "In your face, Parker!"

Most men might have found this aspect of her personality a turn off. I didn't. The shimmy she did along with those borderline-obnoxious victory yelps was cute and hella sexy.

Suppressing a smile, I touched a forefinger to the top of the cleavage tantalizingly displayed by the V-neck of her shirt. "I only lost to you by a stroke, so you were more like l-u-c-k-y."

She harrumphed. "Let's see, I won the go-cart race and just embarrassed you at miniature golf."

"What about my breaking out a can of whup ass on you at the arcade? My two-year-old niece could've hit more baskets than you blindfolded." I shook my head. "It was sad."

"You only won because you're taller and your arms are longer."

I gave her a faux pitying glance.

"Whatever gets you through the night, Ms. Sinclair."

"Don't try to throw me off my game with trash talk." She shrugged off my taunts. "I'm only one win away from taking that medal in your truck home with me today. So why don't you just give up now, hand it over, and kiss the ring?"

She held up a fist.

"You're not wearing one."

What I wanted to do was kiss that fresh mouth of hers. Kiss her until she admitted she didn't just like me, she was crazy as hell about me. It pretty much summed up the way I felt about her.

Riley frowned at her ring-less hand. "Oh, you get the point."

"I think everyone around us got it. Come on, let's go before the manager throws you out. She's already giving you the stink-eye."

Even with Riley insisting we stop by her place first to grab her ball and shoes, it was a short drive from the family fun center to the bowling alley. She tapped the gold medallion swinging from my rearview mirror as I parked. "Take a good look at it, Parker, because the next time you see this medal, I'll be wearing it."

Rounding the SUV, I held open the passenger-side door for her. She gave me a skeptical glance as she hopped down to the pavement. "Are pulling out chairs and holding doors open for me an attempt to get in my head, so I'll lose to you?"

"No, it's what any man who's worth a damn does for a lady."

It was a shame that apparently not enough of them had done it for her.

Riley snorted. "I'll bet this gentleman thing has women wrapped around your pinky finger. Not me though. I still can't stand you, Parker."

Her declaration would have been more effective if she hadn't been pressing her lips together to stifle a grin. I saw the truth in her eyes.

"But you are enjoying our date so far, right?"

She smiled broadly. "I can't remember the last time I had so much fun."

"That's good enough for now. Let's hope I grow on you by the time the day is over."

Inside the bowling alley, I pulled some bills from my wallet and handed them to the teenager behind the counter. The transaction was interrupted when the manager emerged from a tiny office and did a double take. Old man Hadley removed his glasses and wiped the thick lenses with the bottom of his shirt before putting them back on his face.

He knew the both of us, and he was also familiar with the rivalry between our construction companies' bowling teams.

"Y'all playing together, just the two of you?" he asked, apparently not trusting his eyes.

"Yep." I nodded once, confirming it.

"You sure you want to do that, son?"

Again, I nodded.

He inclined his head, which was covered with more salt than pepper hair, in my date's direction. "You of all people should know things could go bad real quick if Riley starts losing."

"Doesn't matter," she said. "Because I'm not *going* to lose."

"We'll see," I told her.

Then I turned to Hadley. "There's nothing wrong with a little healthy competition, after all."

Hadley shook his head and laughed. "That's exactly what her Daddy used to say, and then he'd buy her ice cream for beating the pants off the other kids in the youth bowling league. The worse she beat 'em, the bigger her bowl of ice cream. Sometimes the bowl was bigger than her head."

Riley's lips twisted into a smirk. "Just make sure the snack bar is stocked with plenty of vanilla fudge ripple, because when I finish laying the smackdown on Parker here, I'm going to eat a bowl bigger than a backyard swimming pool."

"The only thing you'll be eating is crow," I retorted as we made the short trek to the lane Hadley had assigned us at the far end of the bowling alley. "Despite letting you have your way with me in my office, I won't go easy on you. The only one getting the pants beat off of them today is you."

I stopped abruptly.

"What?"

"Speaking of pants..." My voice faded out, while my gaze drifted to her jeans, and back to her face. "Are you wearing panties this afternoon?"

Riley met the question with a scowl, but devilment sparked in her eyes. I caught a glimmer of the brazen badass who'd grabbed me by the waistband, unzipped my jeans, and gave me notice that the sex had better be good.

"Maybe I am..." She arched a brow. "Maybe not?"

It was my turn to frown. "No fair. How am I supposed to bowl looking at your behind in those jeans while speculating about what you're wearing, *or not wearing*, underneath?"

She wagged a finger at me. "Nobody ever said life was fair, Parker."

"Riley."

"What?"

"Shut up and bowl."

Three games later, I'd won two, but she'd managed to goad me into extending our match into the best three out of five. Maybe not my smartest move. It allowed Riley to catch up, and now we were even, having won two games each. The tie-breaking game was about to begin.

Both of us were on a roll. I glanced up at the scoreboard on the monitor while Riley hefted her glossy blue ball and stepped up to take her turn. Halfway into the final game, a row of *x's* representing strikes stood next to each of our names. We were dead even, and then Riley broke her streak of strikes.

One pin wobbled, but refused to fall like the rest.

"Damn," she muttered. Then she grumbled a few more colorful words after missing the spare with her second roll.

"Aw, that's too bad." My words held zero sincerity. I'd meant what I'd said earlier about not letting her win. I had my pride, too. Fisting my hand, I held it a few inches from her face as she walked past me. "Looks like *you'll* be the one kissing the ring."

"You're not wearing one." Her eyes narrowed, and I may have spotted wisps of steam coming from her ears.

I walked over to the ball rack. "Just be prepared to pucker up."

"Whatever you say." There was an unfamiliar dulcet quality to her voice that made me suspicious. I didn't know what was going through her head, but figured I'd find out soon enough.

Brushing off the thought, I felt cocky enough to break out my curve shot. My opponent was standing nearby instead of seated behind me. "Watch and learn."

I lined up the shot, confident of rolling another strike. My form was perfect. The ball was seconds from leaving my hand.

"No panties, Parker."

My mouth dropped open just as the ball slipped from my grasp and dropped directly into the gutter.

"Gutter ball!" Riley announced the obvious with a shit-eating grin.

Recovering from her ill-timed revelation, I spun toward her. "And you had to pick *that* moment to divulge your underwear status?"

She shrugged, the smile never leaving her face.

"You got me, good, but it won't happen again."

She'd played her trump card. Nothing else she could say would trip me up now. I snatched my recovered ball from the rack and lined up what was sure to be a strike.

"No panties, *and a fresh, smooth Brazilian,*" Riley said loud enough for only me to hear.

Just as the ball left my hand, my mind flashed to the moment she'd lost the bottom half of her dress in my office. Once again, it rolled right into the gutter. I turned to Riley, and she quickly averted her eyes, looking toward the ceiling.

"Don't play innocent. That was wrong, and you know it."

"I was only making small talk." Snickering, she checked out the scoreboard. "It's not my fault your game is so weak that you can't focus."

Ignoring the annoyed look on my face, she

sauntered past me and snatched her ball from the rack. I waited patiently; my timing had to be as impeccable as hers.

"I've got just the place for you to sit that panty-less Brazilian." My voice was low, but she'd heard me all right. "And as you already know, there's nothing *weak* about my tongue game."

We both watched her ball slip from her hands and roll slowly down the gutter, not even close to the standing pins.

Riley spun on me now. "B-but, but that wasn't fair," she sputtered.

"Nobody ever said life was fair." I mimicked her voice and wagged a finger at her, just like she'd done when the shoe was on the other foot.

She ended the frame with a second gutter ball. I hoped memories of what I could do to her with my tongue had left her discombobulated, just like I felt every time she was near.

We finished the fifth and final game, and I managed to eke out a win. It came as no surprise that my date wasn't pleased with my victory.

"I nearly won, but you had to go remind me about that damn magic tongue of yours," she grumbled as we walked back to my SUV.

I held open the passenger-side door for her. She was staring at the medallion as I slid behind the wheel. "I certainly didn't expect these games to end with us tied."

Turning on the engine, I cranked up the AC but didn't make a move to leave the bowling alley parking lot. Another thing I'd carried out of my marriage, besides scars from someone trying to change me, was a surefire way to get off an annoyed woman's bad side.

"You hungry?"

Hours had passed since lunch, and our afternoon competition had left my stomach growling.

She glanced at me. "I could eat."

Worked every time.

"Pizza?" I remembered it was also her favorite.

"Definitely."

Somehow our decision to go to a pizza restaurant turned into a debate over which one of us could make the best pie. The next thing I knew we were going on a trip to the grocery store and we had a new tie-breaking event for today's competition—pizza making.

"All I'm saying, is that once you taste the blend of spices I put in my pizza sauce, you'll be begging for the recipe." I took the exit off the interstate closest to my house.

Riley crossed her arms over her chest. "Humph. They key to great pizza is in the crust. It has nothing to do with the sauce. Shows how much *you* know."

There was something about a woman who said exactly what she meant. Other men complained Riley had too many rough edges that they found intimidating, but it was those raw, honest, prickly edges that bulldozed their way into my heart.

I turned down my street and blinked at the sight in my driveway. "Well, hallelujah."

"Glad you're finally seeing things my way, Parker."

"Hardly." I spared my passenger a glance. "It looks like I have company."

My brother-in-law Will was loading suitcases into the open trunk of the Mercedes I'd bought Caryn when she'd started college. I parked behind him, jumped out, and got Riley's door.

"Good to see you, man." I shook Will's extended hand.

He glanced at the suitcases. "I'll bet."

"So who..."

"Ended the standoff?" Will finished my question.

"I did."

My sister walked out from behind me and clasped her husband's hand.

Caryn must have noted my surprised expression, because she quickly filled me in. "I began to see myself in Fiona. Too much of me, and it's not the kind of example I want to set for my daughter," she said.

Will stared adoringly at his wife. "I booked a flight to Nashville the second I heard your sister's voice on the phone."

"And don't you dare tell Mom she was right," Caryn said. "I'll never hear the end of it."

"She won't hear it from me," I assured her.

My sister's attention had already shifted to the woman beside me, so I introduced Riley to my family.

"It appears I'm in the wrong again," Caryn said. "When my brother told me about the date he'd planned for you two, I advised him against it."

"You're kidding, right?" Riley grinned at my sister, and then to my surprise, she did the same to me. "I had a great time. The only thing that would have made it perfect is winning that medallion."

"So my brother won?"

Riley shook her head. "Actually, we're tied."

I rubbed my chin. "You guys don't have to leave right away, do you?"

"We need to get on the road soon." Caryn looked at her husband for confirmation.

"What's up?" Will asked.

"We could use some judges for the tie-breaking event of our little competition," Riley explained. "You two like pizza?"

Will released Caryn's hand and draped his arm around her shoulder. "We can stay a little while longer."

Riley and I carried our groceries inside, and she quickly made herself at home in my kitchen. Caryn and Will were seated at the table, and Fiona, who had awakened from her nap, was snuggled in her father's lap.

Soon the entire house was filled with the yeasty scent of rising dough and tomato sauce simmering on the stove.

Will inhaled. "When are those pizzas you two keep bragging about going to be ready?"

"Not for a while yet. We aren't even at the oven stage," I said.

Caryn retrieved a cereal bar from the box in the cabinet and tossed it to her husband. "This ought to hold you over until they're done."

"How am I supposed to eat this when your brother and his girlfriend are teasing my stomach with the smell of *real* food?" Will frowned as he peeled the wrapper off the bar.

My gaze instinctively shifted to Riley. I'd expected her protest to be instant and vehement. Instead, she poked at her pizza dough.

My sister gave her husband a playful swat on the arm. "You'll survive."

"It's not Will's fault he can't resist the tantalizing aroma of my tomato sauce," I insisted.

A snort sounded from the other end of my kitchen island, where Riley was still checking on the lump of dough. "Don't let the smells coming from that pot fool you. Smell is one thing, taste is another."

"Wanna bet?" I asked.

Riley shook her head. The look on her face was downright smug. "I already plan to leave here with that gold medallion. I don't want to take your money, too."

Grabbing a teaspoon from the cutlery drawer, I dipped it into the saucepan, and then held it out to her. "Taste."

"I don't need to taste that inferior sauce. I could probably get better from a dented can in the grocery store discount bin. In fact, I'll bet…"

"Riley!" I interrupted her rant. "Shut up."

Our eyes connected, and for one heated moment, we were back in my office where I'd been a breath away from kissing her. I wanted to kiss her *now*, badly.

"Now taste."

She finally leaned in and wrapped her mouth around the proffered spoon. Her eyes never left mine. Instinctively, I knew she wasn't thinking about pizza, either.

"Did I hear right?"

Riley blinked as Caryn's question dragged us back to the present moment.

"Because I thought I just heard my brother say 'shut up,' and you did."

My sister continued. "Dang it. I just *knew* you weren't the type to fawn all over him."

Will gave his wife a pointed look. "Not your business."

"But…" Caryn began.

"It's a private joke."

I was talking to my sister, but my gaze was trained on Riley. "Isn't that right?"

Riley chuckled softly and a flush warned her light-brown skin. "Yeah, private," she whispered.

"We've got those jokes, too." Will cleared his throat and reached across the table to pat his wife's hand. "In fact, why don't we go into the other room and make sure we have all of your stuff packed? It'll give the chefs time to work."

Caryn frowned. "I'm already all packed. Besides, I thought we were going to all play cards while the pizzas baked?"

"Change of plan." Will gave me a knowing smile before he stood and tugged his wife's hand. Then he hoisted Fee up onto his hip and led his family into the other room.

Unfortunately, their exit didn't bring back the moment.

"So what do you think?"

"Of what?" Riley asked, clueless.

I glanced at the spoon she now held. "The sauce."

"As much as I want to tell you that it sucks, I can't lie." She sighed. "It's pretty damn good, Parker."

"Told you." I took the tasting spoon from her hand and dropped it into the dishwasher silverware rack.

She spread a handful of flour over her workspace. "That doesn't mean it's good enough to win."

"We'll see what the judges say."

Riley grunted. "I just hope they aren't biased, seeing as how they're all members of your family."

The sound of approaching feet and Fiona's appearance in the kitchen forestalled my reply. My niece ran past the kitchen table and rounded the island. I crouched on my haunches and prepared to catch her when she leaped into my arms, but she ran right past me. She stopped in front of Riley and stared up at her instead.

Will stood in the entryway, an apologetic expression on his face. "They're busy cooking, Fee," he said. "Come sit with Mommy and me. We'll come back when dinner's ready."

"It's okay," Riley told him. Then she looked down at the toddler. "Want to help me make pizza?"

Fiona bobbed her head enthusiastically and beamed up at Riley, who scooped her off the floor. Her laugh bounced off the wooden beams on the ceiling as Riley held her over the sink and helped her wash her hands.

Afterward, she sat Fiona on the countertop. "I need you to pound on this dough and help me get it into shape." Riley demonstrated, and my delighted niece followed her lead.

I couldn't help check out the two of them as I worked on my own recipe. Fiona was babbling on and Riley was taking the conversation as seriously as if she were discussing a major project with a client. My niece was already nuts about Riley, and I couldn't blame her. I was, too.

Riley began to spread pizza sauce over the

flattened dough, and Fiona added the toppings. She praised the toddler's clumsy handiwork. "That's perfect. Thanks to you, I think this is going to be the best pizza ever."

"And *I* think I just lost my home court advantage."

Riley shrugged. "Losing to me is something you'd better become accustomed to, Parker."

Will and Caryn had already rejoined us in the kitchen by the time the pizzas were ready to come out of the oven. My sister had made a salad to accompany the pies, and my brother-in-law put himself in charge of beverages.

Dinner had taken a while, so we all demolished our salads pretty quickly. Fee had sampled a bellyful of the veggies Riley had cut up for her pizza and now sat in her mother's lap nursing a juice box. Will reached for a slice of pizza, but I stopped him. "Judge first, then we'll eat."

"Blindfolds?" Caryn asked.

"That's a great idea," Riley chimed in.

I retrieved two neckties I rarely wore, and Caryn and Will obediently covered their eyes.

Riley bit her bottom lip as the couple sampled slices of both pizzas, which we named A and B.

"My mind's made up," Will finally said.

Caryn exhaled. "I need another bite of Pizza A before I make a final decision."

"On second thought, let me have another taste of Pizza A, too," Will said.

Riley continued to chew her bottom lip. She looked worried that they'd both asked for more of my pizza. I'd warned her back at the grocery store that this was a competition she couldn't win.

"They're both good, but Pizza A is a little better." Will pulled off the necktie covering his eyes.

I smiled broadly and nodded.

We all stared as Caryn continued to chew.

"Well?" I prodded, practically tasting my impending victory.

My niece yanked away the blindfold covering her mother's eyes. "Pick mine, Mama!" she squealed, pointing at Riley's pizza.

Caryn kissed the top of her daughter's curly head. "I'm going with my kid and Pizza B."

Their two votes outnumbered Will's one.

Riley immediately broke out in her second victory dance of the day, made worse by Fee leaping out of Caryn's lap to join her. "I w-o-n!"

When the dancing finally subsided, I surrendered the gold medallion to Riley and we all sat down to eat. Of course, she put it around her neck right away and wore it throughout the meal, which was filled with laughter and good conversation. I had to admit, her pizza *was* delicious, and the crust made me wish I'd paid closer attention so I could replicate it.

"So if Fee hadn't intervened, which pizza would you really have chosen?" I asked my sister as I stood to clear the table.

"She already picked mine, Parker," Riley said. "Geez, don't be such a sore loser."

"Me, a sore loser?" My mouth dropped, incredulous.

Caryn looked from one of us to the other. "Uh-uh. I'm not letting you two drag me into it," she said. "Besides, it's time me, my old man, and my baby hit the road."

Will glanced at the clock on the microwave. "If we leave now, we'll make it home shortly after midnight."

We said our good-byes a short while later. Riley and I stood on the front porch and watched the Mercedes back out of my driveway. I loved my sister, but I was happy to see her reconciled with her husband and headed home.

"You know Fiona pocketed your watch, right?" Riley asked.

I nodded, continuing to stare at the car's taillights as their car disappeared down my block. "She also swiped your medallion."

"Yeah, I know."

"And you let her, after all you went through to get it?"

She nodded. "It's a girl-power thing."

"Are you sure the real reason isn't that deep-down, Riley Sinclair is really a big marshmallow?" I nudged her with my elbow.

"Hell, no," she said softly, her declaration lacking its usual vehemence. "Besides, I lost, so I really can't claim it."

"So you're admitting my pizza was better?"

"Humph. You wish."

A quick tally of the day's wins and losses put her ahead, and I corrected her account. She looked down before facing me. The yellow porch light bathed her face in its warm glow.

"It's not the games," she said. "I beat the pants off you, just like I promised."

It wasn't like her to concede victory. "Then what?"

She remained silent, but I didn't push her. This woman didn't feign coyness or play games. She'd clue me in when she was good and ready.

Finally, she cleared her throat. "When you dared me to go out with you, I promised I wouldn't fall for you," she said. "I was wrong, because I *am* falling, Parker, *hard*."

A grin tugged at the corners of my mouth. I'm sure it looked wide and goofy, but I didn't care. *Riley Sinclair was falling for me.*

She heaved a sigh and glanced at my SUV on the curb. "Well, I should probably head home, too." There was a hitch in her voice that told me she didn't want to go any more than I wanted her to leave.

"So you're just going to drop a bomb like that and run?"

She arched a brow. “Did you have a better idea?”

“Actually, there are several things I’d like to do before I take you home.”

A wicked smile spread over her face, the one she’d worn that day in my office. It reached her eyes and made them sparkle. “Such as?”

“First, I need a moment to relish the win.” Brushing a renegade loc off her face, I tucked it behind her ear and smoothed my knuckles down her cheek.

“And then?”

“This.”

Leaning in, I captured her mouth in a kiss infused with months of longing and deep emotions I wasn’t prepared to acknowledge. She moaned and her arms encircled my neck as my tongue explored her mouth in the same way I wanted to explore her entire body.

Refusing to waste another second, I broke the kiss, scooped her up, and flung her over my shoulder caveman-style.

Her laughter filled my ears. “What are you doing, Parker?” She lifted her head off my back.

“The only place I’m taking you tonight is my bed.” I yanked open the front door and strode through the house in the direction of my bedroom.

“Fine,” she called out. “But I’m not cooking your breakfast in the morning.”

I tossed her onto the middle of my king-size bed. “By the time morning comes, you’ll be too damn tired for breakfast.”

stay."

My teeth sank into my bottom lip, which was still puffy from his kisses. I could still feel the burn where the shadow of his beard had scraped my face and inner thighs. Memories of those kisses and the endearments whispered in the heat of the moment flashed through my mind like game highlights.

"So stay." The deep voice carrying the invitation rumbled through me.

"It's not that simple."

Clearly the levelheaded Riley was doing the talking, because the rest of me wanted to dive right back into that bed.

Parker patted the space I'd vacated beside him. "Talk to me."

I glanced at my state of undress before facing him. "You know if I come over there like this, the last thing we'll do is talk."

He inclined his head toward the closet. "You can borrow my robe, if you'd like."

It held the faint scent of soap. I wrapped myself up in it, and I joined Parker on the bed. He put his arm around me and pulled me close. I wasn't a small girl, but being enveloped in his strong embrace made me feel diminutive and cherished.

He brushed a stray loc off my face, and I rested my head on his chest. "Your hesitance to stay doesn't have anything to do with business or the softball championship, does it?"

"No," I confirmed. "That doesn't mean that they aren't important, though. I fully expect Sinclair to be awarded the contract to build the city hall annex. We're also gonna give Parker Construction a softball beatdown, y'all won't soon forget."

I might be losing my heart, but I hadn't lost my mind.

"We'll see," he chuckled, before his tone turned serious. "How much does the guy you were having dinner with the night I asked you out have to do with your misgivings about us?"

Although I'd expected the question, I wasn't sure how to go about answering it. Etiquette was usually the least of my concern, but how did one go about discussing her feelings for one man when in bed with another?

I searched for the right words, but my delay wasn't lost on Parker.

"You've always told me exactly what you think, Riley," he said. "I don't expect anything less from you now."

Lifting my head from his chest, I repositioned myself so I was facing him. "It's just that..." My voice trailed off, and I averted my eyes.

Parker raised my chin with a fingertip until I met his dark gaze. "What happened to the badass who once told me she made grown men cry?"

She never expected to fall for you.

"You can talk to me, Riley. Nothing you say will change the way I feel about you."

I sighed. "Ian's the kind of guy I always imagined myself with. And I went to extraordinary lengths to get his attention."

True to his word, Parker's expression remained neutral as the whole story tumbled out of my mouth. I told him about my crush, the app, and the makeover inspired by the star of *Hot Mess*. "Aren't you bothered by what I just told you?"

"Yes and no," he answered. "I'm not upset, because I know I'm the one who ignites the fire in you, in and out of bed. Yesterday's laughter and your all-day smile? I did that. It's me you woke up with this morning, and the way you made love to me last night, I know you've never been with him."

He hadn't asked the question, but I answered it anyway. "No, we haven't."

"I watched you two at the restaurant and saw you block yawns with your fist. Frankly, you looked bored as hell."

His assessment sounded a lot like Plum's. After busting my ass to meet Ian, I was compelled to defend our relationship. "I do like him, a lot. Right now, we're just dating, and we're both clear on the fact that we're free to see other people. But in my head, he's the man I see in my future."

Closing my eyes briefly, I exhaled. "But when you and I are together, my whole world turns upside down. I can't keep my hands off you, Hudson. I dream about you. I think about you all the time, no matter how hard I try to get you off my mind."

I think a part of me may even love you.

Before I could brush the notion off as ridiculous, his hand moved to my hair. He fisted a handful of my locs, leaned in, and kissed me. It was a slow, drugging kiss that had the effect of a powerful narcotic. When it ended, I couldn't feel my legs. His dark eyes locked with mine. "Hudson, huh? When did you start using my first name?"

It had just slipped out, but I realized it hadn't been the first time I'd called him that in the past twenty-four hours.

"About two orgasms ago."

A smile tugged at the corner of his mouth, and I kissed it. His face grew serious. "That pretty boy in the suit may be what you think you *want*, but I'm the man you *need*. You don't need an app to impress me. I love every rude, obnoxious, competitive, sore-loser, adorable, fun, fascinating, and over-the-top-sexy thing about you."

I blinked at the word love and couldn't help wonder if he'd used it casually, or if it had meant something more.

"It's only a matter of time before you realize everything you truly want is right in front of your face." Hudson rested a finger against my lips, forestalling my reply. "I'm not usually a patient man, but I think you're worth the wait."

Overwhelmed when I finally spoke, I fumbled for the right words to convey the turmoil of my emotions. "H-Hudson," I stammered. "I'm just not sure of how…"

"Today, I'm only asking you to make one decision," he interrupted.

"What's that?" I asked, hoping it wasn't more than I could commit to at this point.

"Should we stay in bed for the next round, or take it to the shower?" The arm wrapped around me slid beneath the robe, and he pinched my bare bottom. "Your choice."

The mood lightened instantly, and we quickly recaptured the sexy playfulness that had ruled the date neither of us was ready to end. I flung back the covers, exposing his gorgeous and fully aroused body.

"Last one to the shower cooks breakfast!"

A week and a half later, I glared at Plum and my sister, who both feigned shock at the sight of me walking into the coffee shop.

"Well, look who's here." Hope rested a French-manicured hand on her chest as I joined them at the table. "It's my long-lost sister."

"Would that be the same sister who vowed she'd never dump her girlfriends the moment she had a boyfriend?" Plum asked.

Hope cracked her pursed lips. "Make that

two boyfriends."

"Slut," Plum joked. She cut into the slice of lemon cake in front of her with a fork and stuffed a bite into her mouth.

"Ha, ha. You two are hilarious," I deadpanned.

The truth was, between work, softball practice, and dating two men, I *had* been pretty busy. *Hot Mess* was on hiatus until January, so our weekly girls' night had also lapsed. I ordered a frothy coffee concoction before rejoining my friend and sister. Unfortunately, the shop had sold out of cake pops.

"So what have you two been up to?"

"Same old stuff with wedding planning and fiancés that you don't even like," Plum said. "So I'm sure you don't want to hear about it."

"That's never stopped y'all before." I didn't bother denying it. It was only for their sakes that I tolerated Plum's mama's-boy fiancé and my cheap-assed future brother-in-law.

"Well, before now, you didn't have anything going on in the romance department," Hope chimed in. "We want to hear the latest on these two men who have had you booked up every evening."

Plum nodded in agreement. "I think that Delilah Cole app is working *too* well. We practically had to make an appointment to hang out with you tonight."

"Stop exaggerating."

Hope took a sip of her latte. She gave me a pointed look as she sat the mug back on the table. "So what's the latest on *your* hot mess?"

"I'm still seeing both of them." I went on to tell them about the three dates I'd had with Ian last week. We'd gone to the opera, a cocktail party thrown by one of his business contacts, and a fundraiser for the city's zoo. The days I hadn't gone out with Ian, I'd spent with Hudson, including a weekender in Atlanta to watch a Braves doubleheader. With Ian out of town on business this week, Hudson and I had gone out every single night.

"After sitting home alone so long, I'm enjoying just dating."

"*Just dating*." Plum mimicked my voice and her eyes narrowed as she scrutinized my face. "Yeah, right. That's why you have that frequently-fucked glow," she said. "So did Mr. Perfect finally get some?"

"Goodness, Plum, you're as crude as Riley," Hope scolded. Then she turned to me. "Well, did he?"

I shook my head. "Ian and I haven't gone beyond the kissing stage."

Hope sighed. "What a gentleman."

It wasn't because of a lack of trying on Ian's part. The timing just never seemed right. *Or the fact that you keep stalling.*

"Dayum! Mr. Construction Boss must be putting it down good enough for the both of them."

"Oh, Plum." Hope's tone was full of the censure she usually reserved for me.

I couldn't stop the wide grin quickly overtaking my face. Oh, yeah. Hudson took care of business in the bedroom every night we were together.

"You don't have to confirm it," Plum said. "That smile pretty much says it all." She raised her hand, and I slapped her a high five.

A knowing expression blanketed Hope's delicate features. "He must be doing something right. When I broke the news that we didn't get the contract to build the city hall annex, I expected you to go ballistic, but you took it with uncharacteristic graciousness."

The truth was I'd already known by the time my sister had gotten in touch with me. Hudson had come over to my place to tell me that the third construction company vying for the job had been awarded the contract. It didn't hurt that he'd brought a bottle of wine and cake pops from my favorite bakery as we commiserated over the disappointing news.

While I shared that tidbit with Plum and my sister, I kept what happened afterward to myself. Although I'm pretty sure they could have guessed.

"I don't understand." Hope swallowed a sip of her latte and frowned. "If you and Hudson Parker are going at it like rabbits, then why is Ian still in the picture?"

"Miss Priss makes a good point," Plum agreed.

They both stared at me, putting me on the spot in a way the two men in my life had yet to do. I reminded them that I was just having fun and enjoying the male attention.

"But when you talk about them, I get the impression you're only having fun with one of them, and I'm not talking about sex," Hope said. "Your dates with Hudson sound as if they are tailor-made for you, while the things you do with Ian seem...well..." Her voice trailed off.

"Fine for someone else, but for you they must be dull as hell," Plum piped up.

"But he's my dream crush."

"Not to mention, rich," she tossed in.

Sure, Ian was wealthy, but I had plenty of my own money that I worked damn hard to earn. Hudson did, too. To me, finances were a nonfactor.

People who once looked through me like I was invisible took notice when I was on Ian's arm. The Beyoncé look-alikes were envious of *me* for a change. I had an ego like anyone else, and I couldn't help but enjoy it a little. Actually, *a lot*.

"You won't be able to continue stringing them along forever," Hope warned.

Plum jammed more cake into her mouth and chewed thoughtfully. Swallowing, she pointed her fork in my direction. "She's right, you know. Sooner or later, things are going to come to a head, and you'll have to make a decision."

"First of all, I'm not stringing anybody along. We're all adults, and everyone knows exactly where they stand." Both my friend and my sister looked skeptical. "And I do like Ian. In fact, he's taking me to New York this weekend. We're going to hit up the museums, and even catch a Broadway show."

Plum laughed. "Yeah, those activities sound right up your alley."

"I like culture."

Hope frowned. "But the intramural softball championship is Friday evening."

"Ian's on business in London this week. We're meeting at LaGuardia on Saturday morning. Our flights are scheduled to arrive around the same time, so I'll be able to celebrate Sinclair Construction's win over the three-day weekend."

My explanation didn't smooth my sister's frown lines. "Does Hudson Parker know about this romantic getaway?"

"Not exactly." I studied the white foam in my coffee mug before answering her. "But he knows all about Ian."

"But not your weekend plans?"

Shit, I was in a hot mess. Or on the brink of one if I didn't at least tell Hudson about my plans with Ian. *I didn't want to risk losing him.*

"You'd better start figuring out what and

who you really want, Riley," Plum advised as she stabbed the last bite of cake with her fork. "Because nobody gets to have their cake and eat it, too."

CHAPTER 18

HUDSON

My phone rang, and I glanced at the watch I'd managed to recoup from my niece during the weekend Riley and I had driven to Atlanta for a Braves doubleheader. Alicia's name popped up on the tiny screen. I signaled and made a right turn into the park entrance using one hand, and grabbed my phone with the other.

"I'm not going to make it to the game tonight," she said.

"Everything okay?"

Her attendance at an intramural softball championship was in no way mandatory, but she'd seemed excited about it when we'd spoke at the office. She'd even mentioned bringing her husband and kids to help cheer Parker Construction on to back-to-back championships.

"Two of the kids have one of those twenty-four-hour stomach bugs, which means we'll all have it before the weekend is over." She went on, giving me too much information about what her kids were spewing out of both ends. "So now I'm wishing we'd opted for a house with more bathrooms than bedrooms."

I slid my truck into a parking space closest to the baseball field. "On that note, I'll let you go. Hope the kids feel better by tomorrow."

"Hold on," Alicia said. "I have a question for you."

"Shoot."

"Now that you and Riley are a hot item, are you going to let Sinclair Construction win tonight?"

I grunted. "For someone so smart, that's an incredibly stupid question."

"One you didn't answer."

Of course I loved seeing a smile on Riley's face, and I would do just about anything to put one there, but I couldn't let my team down any more than she could hers. "No, Alicia, I'm not throwing the game. Parker Construction is in it to win it."

We hung up just as I caught sight of a familiar truck in my rearview mirror. *Riley.*

We hadn't seen each other in two days. She'd mentioned hanging out with her girls one night, and the other I'd assumed she was nodding through a date with that suit she was still seeing.

While I wasn't crazy about the idea of her going out with another guy, I knew it was me she thought about the entire time they were together. It wouldn't be long before she realized I was the only man for her.

We got out of our trucks at the same time. She didn't see me initially. Knowing how competitive she was, I figured her head was already in the game. I called her name and watched her brown eyes light up at the sight of me.

Without any preliminaries, I slipped an arm around her waist and hauled her to me. Her body, like everything else about us, was a perfect fit. "I've missed you." I backed up the sentiment with a kiss that showed her exactly how much.

"Me, too," she said breathlessly, when we finally came up for air.

All I wanted to do was kiss her again, but the sound of car doors slamming in the lot reminded me we both had a game to play. I made it clear I intended to pick up where we'd left off later, either at her place or mine.

She averted the eyes that had been glazed over with passion mere seconds ago. "There is something I wanted to mention to you."

I lifted her chin with my fingertip. "You okay?" It wasn't like her to not look me in the eye.

"Yeah, sure. It's just..."

"Now ain't the time to be snuggled up with the enemy, boss." We both turned to see

Sinclair's outfielder, Deke Boyd, approaching. "Y'all can resume this cozy tête-à-tête after the game."

Riley snorted. "Just make damn sure you stay on top of center field tonight."

I reluctantly dropped my arm from around her waist, but her curves remained firmly pressed against me. "What did you want to tell me?" I asked, when Deke was out of earshot.

"It's not a big deal," she shrugged. "We'll talk after the game."

Something still felt off, but I took Riley at her word. She was just nervous about the game she wanted so badly to win. "As long as you keep it short. I've spent the past two nights alone, and I expect you to make it up to me."

"I'll do my best." She smacked me soundly on the ass. "But first, I have a trophy to win back."

I cocked a brow. "As crazy as I am about you, I intend to do everything in my power to make sure that trophy remains in *my* office."

"Pay attention, Parker." She poked me in the chest. "I'm about to give you and those ringers on your team a tutorial on how to win a softball game."

"Oh, so it's 'Parker' now, huh?"

Her pretty eyes sparkled with mischief. "Making love is one thing, winning softball championships is another. So consider this my way of reminding you that once we take the field, *it's on*."

I wrapped my fingers around the one she was jabbing at me, brought it to my lips, and kissed it, confident we'd end the night on a first-name basis.

She sighed. "There you go trying to throw me off my game with sweet kisses and those sexy bedroom eyes."

"I play for keeps, even if it means getting a little dirty." I released her finger.

"That makes two of us." Riley started to walk away, but turned back in my direction. "Oh, I wasn't going to mention it, but since you've already admitted to playing dirty, I'll toss in the fact that I'm not wearing panties."

My gaze automatically dipped below her waist before meeting her eyes again.

"So you just think about *that* when you're up at bat," she said.

Damn, the woman *did* play dirty. She also knew I wouldn't be able to stop thinking about that ass of hers without panties *all game long*.

CHAPTER 19

RILEY

Five innings into the game, Parker Construction had scored three runs to our none. My crew was playing like shit, and if we didn't turn things around quickly, that trophy would indeed sit in Parker's office for another year.

I stretched my arm and waited for their next batter. The sun had set three innings ago, and lights illuminated the field. Unfortunately, our best pitcher had contracted the flu from his kid, so he'd taken a sick day from work and was in no shape to play tonight.

It had meant shuffling our team around and bringing in a benchwarmer to cover right field. Cal was at my usual position at first base.

Thanks to years of Little League and a father who had loved to play catch in the backyard, I could play pretty much any position and had a decent arm. However, my skills on the mound appeared to abandon me every time my rival-turned-lover stepped up to the plate.

Parker had scored two doubles and a three-run homer off me. It was downright embarrassing, but what was I supposed to do? Call in a relief pitcher every time he came up to bat?

I struck out their second baseman and trotted to the dugout as their team took the field.

"What's up with you, Riley?" Cal took the seat next to me as our first batter stepped up to the plate at the bottom of the inning. "I don't remember Hudson Parker getting a hit off you the last time you had to pitch. Now he's practically smacking the cover off the ball."

Deke grunted on the other side of Cal before I could answer. "You must have missed them playing kissy-face in the parking lot before the game."

"Riley and Parker? Get outta here, Deke," Cal said. "You'd better watch it. She'll take a bite out of your hide for lying." He nudged me with his elbow. "Right, boss?"

"I'm not lying," Deke said. "The two of them were so hot for each other, a bucket of ice wouldn't have cooled them down."

I was staring at the field to avoid my project manager's scrutiny. "He's mistaken, right?" Cal asked again.

Heat rushed to my face. While I wasn't trying to keep the fact that I'd been seeing Hudson a secret, I didn't want my team to think I was throwing the game for him. No way would I do that, but my performance so far had certainly made it look that way.

"Pay attention to your game, Deke," I warned. "If you hadn't been out there navel-gazing, you might have caught the damn ball, and Parker wouldn't have scored that last run."

"Catch it? Thanks to your pitch, it sailed right over my head. What did Parker do, wink at you or something?"

Actually, he had. No one else from my team had caught it, or the fact that the nearly undetectable gesture had left my knees the consistency of pudding. Still, I hadn't thrown him an easy pitch. Parker had just gotten lucky.

"Hold on a sec," Cal said. "Deke's on the level about you and Parker?"

I inclined my head toward the field. "You're up, Cal, and Deke's on deck. Think you two busybodies can stop gossiping long enough to bat?"

Grateful for the temporary reprieve, I didn't miss my project manager's curious glance as he left the dugout. I wasn't trying to lose this game. The only thing I was guilty of was being distracted. Why on earth had I made plans to hook up with Parker after tonight's game? I was so busy kissing and flirting with him, it had totally slipped my mind that I'd be on a flight to New York City first thing tomorrow morning to meet Ian.

Cal got a base hit off one of the opposing team's ringers. This one was a biology major from Tennessee State University and a star on their women's softball team. She was *good.*

I scanned the bleachers behind home plate as Deke came up to bat, my mind still straddling the fence between the game and my personal life. Plum's colorful top made her easy to spot, and her warning popped into my head.

You'd better start figuring out what and who you really want, Riley. Because nobody gets to have their cake and eat it, too.

Automatically, my eyes sought out Parker on the field. A navy ball cap bearing his company's emblem covered his short-cropped hair. But it didn't camouflage the well-muscled body I'd come to know as well as my own. My teeth sank into my bottom lip as images of him touching, kissing, and licking me all over bombarded my thoughts.

As if he felt my eyes on him as he held down third base, Parker turned in my direction. I could feel his gaze, and my heart slammed against my chest in response.

After the game, I definitely had to call off any plans I'd made to see him tonight. *Sigh.* There was no way I could spend the night with Parker and then get on a plane tomorrow morning for a weekender with Ian.

"Riley." I blinked at the sound of my name. "You're up next," a teammate said.

"She's busy checking out her man." Deke said. He had struck out, *yet again*, grumbling as he plopped down on the bench.

Standing, I swatted away a mosquito. Too bad I couldn't do the same to Deke. Any other time, I would have ripped him a new one, but I couldn't when he was right for the most part. Parker wasn't my man, but my eyes had definitely been glued to his every move.

Come on, girl. I gave myself a mental kick in the pants. *Get your head back in the game where it belongs.* Grabbing a bat, I stepped up to the plate, promptly swung, and missed the first pitch.

Sweat rolled down my back as the umpire called strike one, and then a second strike moments later. My stance had been off both times, and I had overswung. I bit down on my lip. Dammit, I knew better.

Two outs for the team, and now two strikes on me.

"Let's go, Riley!" Plum yelled from the bleachers.

I tapped the bat against home plate and set into my batting stance. I gave myself a pep talk. *You've been hitting balls your entire life, and this is no different.* I remembered that I was John Sinclair's daughter. It was past time for me to start playing like it.

I took a gulp of air. It was laced with the aroma of hot dogs and soft pretzels from the nearby stand, and I slowly exhaled. The ball left the pitcher's hand. I forced myself to relax and block out everything except the ball hurtling in my direction.

See the ball. Hit the ball.

Following the advice my dad had given me long ago, the season he'd coached my Little League team, I executed my swing.

The sound of the ball making contact with the sweet spot of my bat meant I'd finally gotten my mojo back. The ball sailed into the outfield and I ran like hell. I was only vaguely aware of their center and right fielder crashing into each other in a failed attempt to catch it.

I made it to third base seconds before the ball. Parker had attempted to tag me out, but it was too late.

A surge of cockiness accompanied my rediscovered mojo. "Too slow," I taunted him.

He met my barb head-on, licking his lips as his gaze swept over me. "Win or lose, I'm gonna tear that ass up tonight."

Have mercy.

My knees nearly buckled on the spot. Parker's deep baritone had been low enough for only me to hear, but there were enough sparks flying between us for lightning to streak across the night skies.

"Promises, promises," I teased. Then I

suddenly remembered that I'd fully intended to cancel anything we had on for the night.

Shit! I wasn't sure what bothered me more: the fact I was digging myself a deeper hole, or that I wouldn't be in bed with him tonight.

The next player in our lineup stepped into the batter's box, and both Parker and I returned our attention to the game. *Priorities, Riley*, I reminded myself. First I needed to help get some points on the board to somehow pull off a win. I'd figure out my romantic hot mess later. Thank goodness Ian was on the other side of the ocean. Maybe *he* was the man I should cancel on.

My teammate fouled out, ending our chances of scoring a run during this inning. Only one inning remained. I stalked to the dugout to retrieve my glove. Sinclair Construction's only hope of pulling it out now was to step up our defense so Parker's team didn't score any more runs. Then we had to pray hard that when we had our final chance at bat, we did.

Both were long shots. Still, I refused to give up. Our team had come too far to lose it all now. Half of our problem was solved when the first two batters on Parker's team fouled out and struck out. I caught a pop-up fly ball for the last out.

It was crunch time now, and we all knew it. Unfortunately, the three weakest hitters on our team were leading off.

"Come on, Al!" I yelled. "Get a hit!"

In what felt like seconds, Al was back on the bench with the first out under his belt. Ditto for the batter who came after him. Two outs. I began to mentally prepare myself for Parker Construction winning back-to-back championships, and the fact that he would be holding on to the trophy I desperately wanted for another year.

Cal nudged me with his elbow. "It's not over yet, boss. Keep the faith."

I nodded and forced a smile. Even if our next batter managed to get on base, there was no guarantee Cal, Deke, or I wouldn't be the third out, ending the game and costing us the championship.

Resisting the urge to start packing up my things for the season, I watched our second baseman step up to the plate and take a swing.

"Oh, my God! He got a hit!" Standing up, I clutched Cal's arm in excitement. "We've got a man on base!"

He grinned back at me. "We're down, but not out."

He was up next. I released his arm and gave him an encouraging slap on the back. Cal winced. "Damn, Riley. That hurts!"

"Just get a hit, tender ass!"

The entire dugout laughed at my quip, buoyed by the sliver of hope we had of pulling this out. Our excitement escalated when Cal managed to get a walk on a full count. We had two men on base, and now it was Deke's turn to bat.

"Do your best," I said, not wanting to add to the pressure he faced. "That's all I ask."

He nodded, and then side stepped me. "No offense, but I'm still seeing a chiropractor from that slap on the back you gave me for hitting the first home run of the season," he joked.

Shutting my eyes tight, I crossed my fingers when Deke entered the batter's box. "I can't look, y'all." But I couldn't help peeking after everyone around me began to cheer.

"Back-to-back walks, and the bases are loaded!" Our team's left fielder slapped me a high five.

We also had two outs. It was all on me now, and after riding my team so hard all season long, I didn't want to let them or myself down. I heard two high-pitched squeals as I stepped up to bat, and I smiled knowing both my sister and Plum had my back regardless of the outcome.

See the ball. Hit the ball.

I chanted the mantra under my breath. Each time I repeated the words, my jitters subsided and my confidence increased. The pitcher threw the ball, and I leaned into the swing, giving it my all.

I knew it was a good hit the moment I heard my bat smack the ball, which seemed to disappear into the night sky. I didn't waste time staring at it, and took off running as fast as I could, tagging first base, then second, and then running right past Parker. He was shouting frantically at a teammate who had tripped over his own feet, trying to get the ball, to throw to home plate.

I crossed home before the ball, which meant I had got an inside-the-park grand slam home run. We had won! My teammates swarmed me as it sunk in. After playing six innings of mediocre softball, we'd come through in the seventh and actually won the championship.

While I happily accepted the congratulations, hugs, and pats on the back that accompanied victory, my gaze sought out one person. *Hudson.* I peered over the shoulders of my teammates until I finally saw him walking toward me with a huge smile on his face.

Breaking away from the hoard of well-wishers, I sprinted toward him. His smile grew even wider as I closed in on him. My cap fell off, freeing my locs, and I leaped into his arms.

"Congratulations on the win." He swung me around, and my feet dangled above the ground.

When he stopped, I stayed in his arms with my hands braced against his biceps. My head was still spinning like it did every time I was near him.

"You're not mad?"

He shook his head. "Just the opposite. While I wasn't going to let you win or make it easy for you, when *you're* happy, *I'm* happy." His expression softened, and he tucked a wayward loc behind my ear. "I'm more than just crazy about you, Riley Sinclair. *I love you.*"

His declaration filled me with emotions I had yet to put a voice to. "And I love…"

"Hey, Riley!"

Flinching, I stopped midsentence and turned at the sound of my name being called by a familiar voice. It couldn't be, I thought, but sure enough, Ian was striding across the field in our direction.

"You were about to say?" Hudson prompted.

Confusion muddled my thoughts. "I-I don't know," I whispered as Ian joined us.

"Congrats on the game." Ian hugged me and planted a kiss on my forehead. Dressed in khakis and a coral polo shirt, he looked like he'd gotten lost searching for his country club golf foursome.

"W-what are you doing here?" I asked. "I thought you wouldn't be back in the country until tomorrow."

Ian smiled. "I finished my business and jumped on an earlier flight to surprise you. I arrived just in time to watch you cross home plate with the winning run."

"Um, that's great," I choked out.

"Now we can fly to NYC for our weekender

together, instead of you meeting me there tomorrow. And I was able to snag tickets to that hit Broadway show *Franklin*, everyone's talking about. It's based on one of the country's founding fathers. Is that cool or what?"

"I didn't know you had plans for the weekend," Hudson said.

Facing him, I opened my mouth, but no words came out. Meanwhile, Ian went on and on about the romantic trip he'd planned to the city. Hudson's face was impassive, but the hurt in his eyes cut me to the core.

The man had just confessed he was in love with me, and I think I was about to tell him the same thing until Ian had come along. Now I didn't know what to say.

"You look familiar." Ian narrowed his eyes at Hudson, as if he were trying to place him. "Have we met before?"

Hudson shrugged. "I don't think so," he answered Ian, but his gaze questioned me.

For a woman who always had something to say, right now I had nothing. Dating and having fun had suddenly become heavy and complicated.

He waited a few beats before slowly shaking his head. Apparently, my silence had been all the answer he needed. His gaze flicked to Ian before he stared pointedly at me. The hurt I'd detected in his eyes just moments ago was replaced with remoteness. It was if he were looking at a stranger.

"Congrats on the win, Riley. You two enjoy your weekend," he said, then turned and walked away.

I stared at his back as he walked over to the dugout with a few of his teammates.

"He seemed to take the loss well." Ian was talking about the game, of course. He had no idea of the real loss he'd just witnessed.

"Yeah, Hudson's a good man," I said softly.

Hope and Plum, who had been standing nearby, joined us. My sister automatically reached for my hand to give it a quick squeeze.

"Everything okay?" Plum asked.

Nodding, I swallowed the lump of emotion rising in my throat. I pasted a smile on my face and proceeded to introduce Hope and Plum to Ian.

"You two headed over to First Down to celebrate?" Plum asked.

"Sorry, but I can't." Ian turned to me. "I came straight here from the airport. I need to take care of a few things at home and pack a bag for the weekend." He leaned in and kissed me on the cheek. "I'll pick you up first thing in the morning."

He was barely out of earshot before my sister and friend were clamoring to find out what had just gone down.

"While technically I've been single all this time, it feels like I've just been dumped." If I were the type of woman who cried, I'd be bawling my eyes out right now.

My sister wrapped an arm around my shoulder. “We don’t have to go to First Down.”

“If you want, I can pick up a bottle of wine, a couple dozen cake pops, and meet you at your house for a break up pity party,” Plum offered.

It was tempting to hide out at home with my girls, but I owed it to the team to put in an appearance at the sports bar, even if I was no longer in the mood to celebrate.

CHAPTER 20

HUDSON

First Down was the last place I wanted to be tonight.

If it was just about me, I'd go home, plop down on the sofa in front of my big TV, and watch my favorite MLB team screw up their chances of getting a wild card berth. But I had a long three-day weekend to mope, and tonight was for Parker Construction's softball team. Despite our loss tonight, we'd had a hell of a season.

After buying food and a round of beers, I stood with a few of the guys from both teams watching the baseball game on a television near the bar. Julie was working tonight, but I shut down her flirting with one glance. She was flat-out gorgeous, but right now, even indulging in a mindless fuck felt like too much effort. Besides, my heart still belonged to a woman who didn't want it.

"Thought we were on our way to back-to-back championships," my company foreman said. He roused me out of my thoughts. "Who would have thought Sinclair would rally in the last inning and eke out a win?"

"Biggest last-inning comeback I've seen in a long time." Owen Mills, whose team hadn't made the playoffs, had come out to watch us play. "I knew Riley could ball, but I never thought she'd drive in four runs in the clutch. I'm impressed."

I nodded. Although it had cost us the game, deep-down I'd been proud as hell of her. Still, it would be a while before I could hear Riley's name without feeling a sharp ache. I'd believed she was on the brink of telling me she loved me earlier. Turned out I was just a damn fool.

Another member of my crew chimed in and clinked his beer bottle against mine. "We'll get the championship back next year."

"Yeah, we will."

"Not if we can help it." Cal and Deke joined us.

I inclined my head in their direction. "Good game, fellas."

"Thanks, but y'all didn't make it easy for us," Cal conceded. "Not at all."

Deke took a sip from his beer. "Surprised to see you here, Parker. The way you and Riley were going at it in the parking lot before the game, I thought the two of you would have booked a room for the night."

"Don't start that up again," Cal told his

teammate. Then he turned to me. “Deke has got it into his head that you and our boss have some big romance brewing.”

“I know what I saw,” Deke insisted.

It didn’t matter what he’d seen. Not anymore.

“Riley and I are just friends.” That wasn’t exactly true, but it wasn’t any of Deke’s business.

“Yeah, the two of you looked real friendly.”

Cal shrugged. “Let it go, man.”

His advice hadn’t been directed at me, but it applied all the same. It was time to let the idea of me and Riley Sinclair go—once and for all. I heard her name accompanied by a few cheers and glanced toward the entrance to see her sit down at a table with her sister and friend.

I deliberately turned back to the television, but not even the Braves could hold my attention.

You’re going to run into her. Get used to it.

Right now the wound was still too fresh. I’d put in an appearance. My team was enjoying the free food and drinks. I’d just finish my beer and get out of here.

“Hudson, can we talk?”

I was so busy trying to forget Riley that I hadn’t seen her approach. Tilting the bottle to my lips, I took a long swig. “So talk.”

She glanced pointedly at the guys standing around. “In private.”

I shrugged and walked with her to a corner without a television. It was about as private as you could get in a sports bar.

She licked her lips. "I hate the way we left things back at the park."

"So what was your plan? Leave my bed tonight and roll around in his all weekend?" I glanced around us. "Where is he, anyway?

"Hudson, it wasn't like that, I..."

"Save it, Riley." I drained the last of my beer. "I was telling the truth when I told you earlier that I'm happy when you're happy. Congratulations. You have your championship and the man of your dreams."

"But, Hudson..."

I held up a hand to forestall any more of her bullshit explanations. She'd decided what she wanted, and it wasn't me. "Enjoy them both, cause we're done."

CHAPTER 21

RILEY

The next morning, I squirmed in the passenger seat of Ian's Mercedes, trying and failing to block out the strains of the Broadway soundtrack filling the car's interior.

"*Franklin* has been sold out for months." Ian bobbed his head in time with the music as he followed the signs on the interstate leading to the airport. "Fortunately, I was able to call in a few favors for tickets." He made it sound like he'd just won the lottery.

"Great."

Hope had talked about this show ad nauseam. She'd flip her shit if she knew I was seeing it tonight. I stifled a yawn with my fist.

Ian must've caught the gesture in his peripheral vision. "If there's something else you'd rather listen to, feel free to change the station."

I jumped at the offer, and moments later I settled into the butter-soft seat as last night's baseball scores replaced songs that pretty much sounded all the same to me.

"Just you wait," Ian said. "Once we see the show, you'll be hooked on the soundtrack, too."

The innocuous comment sounded familiar. I'd been telling myself a version of the same thing all night. Actually, for weeks now.

Just you wait. Once you spend more time together, you and Ian will find things you have in common.

The truth was, we hadn't.

Just you wait. Once you go out with Ian a few more times, passion will spark.

The truth was, it hadn't.

Then there was the thought that had replayed in my head throughout the sleepless night.

Just you wait. Once Ian picks you up in the morning, you'll want to go on this trip. He's the man of your dreams. He'll make you forget you've fallen in love with Hudson.

Shifting in my seat, I turned to the man I'd went through so much trouble to be with. I tried to summon the longing I'd felt when I'd stood in front of the Espresso building site watching him earlier this summer.

His classically handsome profile didn't stir anything in me beyond friendship. I didn't need Delilah Cole or an app to know this trip wouldn't change that, or the fact that I loved someone else.

The thought of Hudson brought a bittersweet smile to my face as memories from the last few weeks bombarded me. Hot sex against his office wall. His risking a big contract to stop and change my tire. Our sexy and hilariously competitive first date. Romantic subsequent dates. His smile. His scent. His touch.

There wasn't anything I didn't love about Hudson Parker, and now I'd lost him because I'd been too damned stupid to see what was right in front of my face.

Regardless, I couldn't compound one mistake by making another.

Ian slowed the car to a stop at the airport's valet parking section. A young man was already standing at the driver's side of the car with a clipboard when I placed my hand over Ian's.

"I'm sorry, but I can't go to New York with you."

A frown creased his perfect features as he stared at me. "Aren't you feeling well?" he asked. "I noticed you haven't said much this morning, but I assumed it was because of the early hour."

I shook my head. "No, I'm fine. It's just..."

"Hold on, are you breaking up with me?" His jaw dropped and disbelief registered in his eyes. "Now?"

The valet parking attendant knocked on the driver-side window, and Ian dismissed him with a flick of his hand.

"Technically, no. You're the one who said we were just having fun. You were very clear on the fact that we weren't a couple and were free to see anyone else we pleased."

"I know what I said, but…" He paused, and I could see the moment it all came together in his head. "It's that guy you were talking to after the game, isn't it?"

I nodded.

"Damn. I *thought* I was getting some odd vibes from you two last night, but I told myself it was just the jet lag playing tricks on me."

"I'm sorry, Ian. You're a great guy, and I like you a lot, but if you think about it, we don't have that much in common. Or any chemistry."

"We've been trying to force something that doesn't exist." He sounded like he was talking to himself more than to me.

I nodded again and apologized for the timing.

"We're going to miss a great show, and it's sold out through next year." He exhaled. "I'll take you home."

He moved to put the car into gear, but I stopped him. "You go on and enjoy *Hamilton*."

"*Franklin*," he corrected.

Whatever. I shrugged. "I'll call Uber or grab a cab home."

"You sure?" Ian asked. He didn't stop me

when I grabbed my bag from the backseat and got out of the car. Instead, he tossed his car keys to the attendant and ran through the airport doors, not bothering to look back.

I stared out the window of the hired car as I headed home, thinking about the love I'd lost, and wondering if there was anything I could do to get it back.

During my rivalry with Hudson, I'd never shied away from him, or a challenge. That's why I stood at his front door two days later. It was Monday morning, the last day of the three-day weekend.

I sucked in a deep breath to gather my courage, and then rang the doorbell. I could hear the sound of heavy footsteps approaching on the other side of the door. The knots in my stomach pulled tighter, and my palms were perspiring so hard the plastic bag in my hand threatened to slip from my grasp. Two days of thinking, and I hadn't come up with any magical words to turn back time. Nor erase the fact that I'd hurt him.

All I could do now was offer a heartfelt apology and finally say the words I should have said to him two days ago. *I love you.* Not that they would matter now. The damage had been done. But I owed it to both of us to lay everything on the table.

The door swung open and Hudson's eyes brightened at the sight of me. The tiny gesture filled me with hope. Unfortunately, it was short-lived. His face quickly turned to stone. I pressed my lips together. What did I expect?

Crossing his arms over his chest, Hudson leaned against the doorjamb. "What do you want?"

"There are some things I need to say. Can I come in?"

He stared at me, and I noticed his face looked haggard. His eyes were cold. Finally, he pushed off the doorjamb and stepped aside. No words, but I figured it was as close as I was going to get to being invited in. The heels of my shoes sank into the plush carpet as I entered the living room.

I glanced around as he closed the door behind me. I couldn't help but remember the fun evenings and sexy nights I'd spent in this house. A place where I'd once felt welcomed. In a short time, I had grown to know it as well as my own home.

"How was New York? You and what's-his-name enjoy yourselves?"

"I didn't go," I said softly.

He blinked, but his face remained hard. "Too bad. Maybe y'all can get a rain check."

"Ian went, but I didn't. I couldn't."

The scowl on Hudson's face deepened. "If you've had your say, feel free to leave."

"That wasn't what I came here to tell you."

"Spit it out, Riley. So we can both get on with our day."

"I'm so, so sorry I hurt you. If I had it to do again, I would have shouted how much I love you from the top of my lungs."

He shook his head. "I'm nobody's second choice. You made your decision, now live with it. I hope you and that pretty boy are..."

"Shut up, Parker!"

His dark eyes widened. Using the element of surprise, just as he'd done with me that day in his office, I shifted the bag I was holding to my other hand and touched my fingertips to his lips.

"Listen to me. I was wrong and stupid. It's like when potential homeowners are looking at a new construction. They focus on cosmetic things like flooring, cabinets, paint colors, and shiny new appliances. They overlook the most vital thing, the foundation, when it's really what gives a home life."

Removing my fingers from his lips, I pinned him with a gaze. "In my heart, you were never second best. *You're my foundation, Hudson Parker. You give me life. Now I'm pleading with you to give me another chance.*"

My next breath left my body in a whoosh as he hauled me into his arms. He lowered his lips to mine and bestowed them with the gentlest and sweetest of kisses. "I love you, too." His breath fanned against my face as he spoke, and then he smiled. "But I have two questions."

"Ask me anything," I said, savoring the feel of being back in his arms again.

He dropped a kiss on my forehead. "It's eighty degrees outside. What's with the trench coat? And what's in that bag you're holding?"

"Oh, that." I laughed and took two steps backward. Working around the bag in my hand, I undid the belt on the coat and let it drop to the floor.

Hudson's eyes nearly popped out of his head at the sight of me in nothing but an apron and high heels. I pulled the carton of eggs from the bag. "I'm here to cook breakfast." I licked my lips. "You eating?"

He cocked a brow. "Definitely."

Pivoting on my heels, I made an about-face that put my bare ass on full display and sashayed past the kitchen in the direction of his bedroom. *"Then come and get it."*

CHAPTER 22

Five Months Later

RILEY

Hope shook her head at me in disgust. "Oh, Riley. Must you always be such a bad sport?"

"I'm still here, aren't I?"

Rolling my eyes at my sister, I looked on as Parker's team was presented with the league's championship bowling trophy. Another bowling pin made out of crystal. It was beautiful, but I'd wanted it to join the softball trophy currently residing in Sinclair Construction's offices.

Still applauding, Plum nudged me with an elbow. "Hope makes a good point. Now clap and show your man some love. It isn't like you won't be able to visit that crystal pin whenever you want. You and Hudson are practically inseparable."

I gave a half-assed clap and suppressed a smile. My friend was right. Hudson and I had been going strong since the morning I'd showed up at his place to cook breakfast. To this day I didn't remember ever making it to the kitchen.

After posing for a few photos with the trophy, Hudson passed it on to his teammates and joined us. He looked from Hope to Plum. "Are you two giving my woman a hard time?" He kissed me on the lips. "She can't help being a sore loser."

Hope shook her head. "Don't encourage her."

"I suggest you sleep with one eye open," Plum said. "Otherwise, Riley might swipe that sparkly new trophy of yours."

"Give me a break, I'm not that bad," I laughed, looking on as my sister and my friend exchanged glances. Neither looked convinced.

I turned to Hudson. Despite the jovial mood surrounding us, his face was serious and he stared deep into my eyes. His fingertips grazed my cheek as he brushed a loc off my face.

"I love you so much," he murmured softly. Then he reached into his pocket and retrieved a black velvet box. He popped it open, and I gasped at the sight of the most beautiful diamond solitaire I'd ever seen.

"It's no trophy or crystal pin, but this ring sparkles and shines with the light of my love, and if you agree to be my wife, I'll always be the real winner. Marry me, Riley."

"I do," I blurted out, and he slipped the engagement ring on my finger.

Plum's high-pitched happy squeal filled my ears.

Smiling, Hope shook her head. "Oh, Riley," she admonished. "You don't say 'I do' until the wedding."

"Make it a big, splashy one," Plum chimed in. "Between Hope and I, we have plenty of bridal magazines."

I looked from my friends to my new fiancé. "I don't care about a big wedding. I'd sooner hop a flight to Vegas."

The man who'd always known me so well plucked his jacket from a nearby chair. He reached into its pocket and pulled out two plane tickets. "That's what I thought you'd say."

A tsk-tsk sound came from my sister's direction. "Oh, Hudson, how positively tacky."

"Lighten up, Miss Priss, and pack a bag," Plum said, grinning. "We're headed to Vegas."

You are cordially invited to
attend the Las Vegas nuptials of
Miss Riley Sinclair and Mr. Parker Hudson.
The happy couple's wedding takes place in
Hope Sinclair's story:

Here Comes the Honeymoon...?

ABOUT THE AUTHOR

A former newspaper crime reporter, Phyllis Bourne writes romantic comedy to support her lipstick addiction. A nominee for Romance Writers of America's RITA® award, she has also been nominated for a RT BOOKReviews Reviewer's Choice Award and won Georgia Romance Writer's Maggie Award of Excellence. She lives in Nashville with an understanding husband, who in one kiss can discern the difference between department store and drug store lip gloss. When she's not at the computer, Phyllis can be found at a cosmetics counter spending the grocery money.

72129798R00145

Made in the USA
Columbia, SC
16 June 2017